KU-616-172

Proud Island

Peadar O'Donnell

THE O'BRIEN PRESS

11 Clare Street Dublin 2 Ireland

First published 1975
The O'Brien Press
11 Clare Street Dublin 2 Ireland.

ISBN 0 9502046 7 6
© Peadar O'Donnell

Printed by E. & T. O'Brien Ltd.
11 Clare Street Dublin 2 Ireland.

Cover Design by Debby Bell
Photo by Pat Langan courtesy of The Irish Times
Book designed by Michael O'Brien

Note for readers outside Ireland
in the text the letters 'T.D.' refer to a member
of the Dail or Parliament in Dublin.

Without as much as by your leave

to two fellow Ulstermen

John Hewitt

and

Micheal MacLaverty

I

A

1

crowded island was a special kind of townland. It was more than a scatter of houses. It was *Our* Island. *This* Island. How could it be else when one night of storm and the boats out made one heart of all its people?

The granite faced western shore, for all its dents and wrinkles, had the sprawling curve of a new moon. The ends of the bend rested on two headlands. A wall of mud and stone — The Rampart — stretched from one headland to the other. The houseless waste West of The Rampart was The Bog, a turbury and grazing commonage. The Rampart was in constant good repair for it was the lore of the island that on the Saturday following St. Patrick's Day every house must send a man to mend any rift or weakness in it. There were three gaps wide enough to let through a donkey bearing two creels and they came in for skilled care, so that they opened and shut easily.

The land east of The Rampart was a patchwork of small fields basted together by short, everyway stone fences. Houses were sprinkled about without pattern beyond being gable-on to the West wind; one storey, thatched, vaguely white with windows in one side wall. A network of dark narrow footpaths wove them together. These paths threaded their way through slits in the stone fences. There was so little space between them that it was not worth while to come abreast; maybe that had something to do with the island way of walking, one on the heels of the other; and a say too in keeping the paths narrow. If the nearest route to door or spring well was through a cropped field the path was there for use — no man would put a spade in one — and again single file suited best. But every footpath, no matter by what criss-cross it got there, fed in the end into one that led to Poolban; nature's gift to the island, a wide safe anchorage able to give shelter to the whole fishing fleet.

On the shoulder of the ridge above Poolban, and set full sideways to the West wind, there was a house. It was likely that any house so placed with traffic going by its gables would be often on people's tongues, but this one sort of swaggered its own way into notice. It was roped and thatched every second year, not every third or fourth like the others. That made sense for it was a house that had much to withstand in a rough winter. A window in the south gable lit a loft; the only loft on the island. But what set it apart most was its whiteness. There was no reason one could see for whitewashing the outer walls every Summer but the habit went back as far as memory and no mocking word was aimed at it. And there was this: The people of that house gave themselves no airs. They were neighbours. They borrowed and they loaned and what better proof than that of neighbourliness could you have?

For all that, the island put its own stamp on that

house at Poolban. Take the man there with the island at its peak. He was Hughie Duffy not Hughie Eoin Rua as he would be on any other floor. His father before him was Eoin Rua Duffy, not Eoin Rua Manus and so on back and back. Even the new woman into the house shed her island name. Hughie's wife, Susan, was not Susan Dan, nor even Susan Hughie but Susan Duffy. And again nobody made a wonder of it.

There was a patch of grass between Hughie Duffy's house and the harbour. It was known as Duffy's Green and was in its own way another commonage. Crews gathered there to smoke and chat before the tide bade them be on their way. Boats put out from there for mass on Sundays. The floating shop put in there every Tuesday.

But even tho' Hughie Duffy owned The Green and was a man of standing among his neighbours — indeed he was outstanding for he was the one man on the island who spent a while in prison and behind barbed wire — still not he but Johnny Anthon had most say on The Green. Johnny Anthon was a bulky bewhiskered, middle-aged man in gansey and corduroys and broken peak cap. He shared his say and sway with Conal Andy who was around his age and his like in bulk and dress except that he wore his cap peak to the back. Then there was Paddy Brian, a dim figure; a shade the eldest. He was light bodied and scarce of words but he had his place with the other two in what the crews named the Three Wise Men. Paddy Brian was clean shaven as became a man who spent a while in Boston. He wore a glaze peak cap.

Susan Duffy sometimes came to the door to fling a word into a noisy argument on The Green.

She was tallish, her black hair in soft coils on top of her head. But it was not to banter she came to the door the morning of the seagulls. She needed more light to thread an overfine needle with a thread which was a shade coarse. If her eyes were busy her ear was free. She heard an angry cluck and knew it was the red hen, peeved because the stable door was shut keeping her from nesting in the manger. She went twice past Susan. 'Chokin' to you, can't you see I'm busy.' Susan heard a step and a 'made' cough and knew without looking up that Kitty Paddy Brian was at hand. She called out to Kitty to open the stable door. Kitty was an ageing stumpy woman with her scarce grey hair in a tight bun held together by a net. She did as she was bid and told Susan she should thank God for a hen that would only lay in a safe place. She had a tramp of a white one, and, as the devil would have it, the best layer in her flock, but careless where she dropped her egg and, to make matters worse, she told the world about it when it was done. It was a race then between Kitty and Conal Andy's dog which would get to the egg first. But that was life for you, if it was not one thing it was another.

The tip of the thread peeped through the eye of the needle and the fingers got a grip. Susan's eyes were now free for she could do the rest by feel; even knot the doubled thread. The rocks were thronged with seagulls but then that was the way since first light. That told that herring shoals were near. Every year it was that way, the seagulls first and the herring shoals two days later. Well, the men of the island were ready. Any need there was for last minute bustle was around haggards.

Susan was about to turn away when her eye

caught a flick of white. It was the under belly of a lone seagull coming in fast. She swept low over the rocks. 'There's always a straggler' Susan said back over her shoulder to Kitty. She was never able to say whether the hurrying seagull made any cry, for one of the lazy greybacks that lived around Poolban scrounging bits of bait and dog fish chose that moment to set up a throaty cry; it could be a cheer or a jeer, she said later.

The seagulls on the rocks, on this their first day of rest, had their bills tucked in under their wings. Susan noticed their startled, raised heads. While you would clap your hands their wings threshed in such a flurry that some birds were pushed into the sea. Susan's gasp brought Kitty to the doorway. The seagulls were now in the air gathering into clusters. They flew off North. Kitty and Susan came outside for a better look. They went to the gable to see if anybody else was seeing. There were heads in doorways and a sprinkling of people at gables. Men on The Green laid down whatever they had in their hands. Here was a thing happening that had not its like in living memory. Noisy women hurried out over the paths to join the men on The Green. They were scared.

2

Johnny Anthon could do little to soothe their unrest. He shared it too much. The like had not been seen ever and no word of it came down from the old people. The seagulls came and the herring followed just as the scribble of snow on the mountains beyond told that winter was at hand. The island and the seagulls rested on the herring. The fear in everybody's minds was that the goings on of that morning meant that the shoals had struck to the North out of reach of oar and sail. There was just one thing: Johnny Anthon found ease in the fact that the seagulls were often three days later than this year so it could be they had only gone a short distance and would be back. Maybe it was that they found themselves too far ahead of the herring shoals. After all, seagulls had to eat. But he didn't quieten anybody's mind for it was clear he had not much belief himself in what he said.

There was no wisdom anybody could call on. It was not something in the sky that scared them away. The island had its good share of skills but put them all together and they could make no sense of this. If the like ever happened it was at some far-off place. There was just one man who might get at its meaning. Hughie Duffy might have talked with fishermen in jail because when he came home it was his firm opinion that the men he was with there would one day run the country and they would give the islands boats and gear on share. But Hughie Duffy was out in the bay. Whistle to make him raise his head and let all the women shake their scarfs.

Hughie waved a hand, finished his chore and rowed towards Poolban.

Kitty Paddy Brian bustled to the front: Did he not see the seagulls? How could he go on fishing like nothing happened when everybody else was half out of their minds? No need to be half out of their minds he told them. For one thing, they had no power over it. It could be that the shoals were taking a new route. He met fishermen in jail who suffered from the like, herring changing their routes, keeping so far out only big boats could reach them. They might not come within reach of oar or sail for years.

'Then what's before this island if the herring turn their backs on us' a woman worried.

There was one thing to bear in mind he told them: People were not seagulls. They could not take wing and away. He glanced towards the open door where Susan stood with the baby in her arms. They made way for him and he passed through the fidgety gathering. 'We'll do something' he said back over his shoulder. 'This is not a bolt from the blue to some of us.' The puzzled neighbours looked after him. Johnny Anthon spoke quietly. 'Conal Andy and myself will take him with us tonight over to Paddy Brian's. Hughie Duffy studies things. It could be he wants time to think. He weighs his words.'

People could see Johnny Anthon had more hope.

Susan stood in the open doorway until Hughie passed through and then she followed and shut the door behind her. Women saw that as a sign they were not wanted. The Three Wise Men held their ground. People still waited for them to move or speak. Johnny Anthon waved them away but they were slow to move. They did not want to be alone with their fears. They urged Johnny Anthon to go in after Hughie and ask him straight out what he meant. It was little short of mocking to say people were not seagulls.

But Johnny Anthon was firm. Hughie would talk when he was ready. It was his opinion that that night in Paddy Brian's would be a memorable one.

3

Johnny Anthon with Conal Andy on his heels walked in on Hughie Duffy's floor before the first fire of the night had time to become red hearted. Susan fussed getting them chairs, tho' she knew full well they were not come to ceili for men didn't pick on a house with a cradle on the floor for that. Johnny Anthon wasted no time in stating his errand. Hughie was the one man among them whose breath wasn't taken from him that morning. If the island was to have a wink of sleep that night he must open his mind and say why he was not upset like everybody else and the place to do that in order to reach the whole island was beyond at Paddy Brian's.

Without any ado Hughie picked his cap off the window sill and led the way out. Paddy Brian's kitchen was thronged, and for the first time there were women on the floor. Way was made for Johnny Anthon to get near the fire. Conal Andy no more than got his heels inside the doorstep. Johnny Anthon spoke for the whole kitchenful. They were worried, and he would even go so far as to say, frightened. They had skills among them from reading the sky to the endless eddies set up by the tides, but put all their skills together and add in all the wisdom that had come down to them from the old people and they had nothing to go on to give a meaning to that morning's happenings. Did the flight of the gulls mean that the shoals were not coming? Nobody on the island ever thought the like would happen. A sprinkle of snow on the mountains was the first breath of winter. The gulls a message from the herring shoals. These things happened. Nobody ever asked why. Here they were now, neighbours together, without a word to say, or rather with only one word to say and that was what frightened them. Hughie Duffy was the only man among them not to be upset.

Hughie was nudged, and sort of squeezed forward so that when he turned he was by Johnny Anthon's side facing the others; a man of light build, tall, a clean shaven weather whipped face. Hughie spoke: It was like a chat; it was a fact he knew men who talked of the like happening on the other islands. Herring changed their route, sometimes only keeping too far out beyond the reach for small craft. It was a thing Peter Dan and himself often talked of. True, the herring were out of reach whether they took a far off course or struck close-in somewhere else. What to do if the like happened was never too clear. Big boats to follow the shoals was one way, but since they were not to hand the only hope was the empty islands a day's rowing to the South West. There were fishing grounds around them. A boat could not go there, fish and get back in one day. He had these islands in mind the time he went to Dublin, bypassing their T.D. Now they must reach these new fishing grounds to take the sting out of the loss of the herring. The only way Peter Dan and he saw to do that would be to put up shelters on the island and spend a week there at a time. Then, too, better use could be made of their fields, especially since limestone and broad leaved seaweed were to hand. Plenty of potatoes and fish were a good foundation. It was too late to do much that season but by the look of the sky it would be safe to go out and raise the huts for next May. As well as build the huts two or three crews could be spared to 'prove' the fishing ground. It was his guess and Peter Dan's that this would be worthwhile.

All of a sudden people seemed to forget they had come together in fear. Now they clamoured and almost cheered; women especially. So their men would be away, grazing out, next Summer. Johnny Anthon raised a hand. 'It's a true saying that the mind of man is a busy place,' but the kitchen was in no mood for discourse from Johnny Anthon. They wanted to hear more from Hughie Duffy and they would not be silenced. Johnny Anthon had to raise his voice; he was on Hughie Duffy's side and all he had to say was that Hughie Duffy while in jail stretched his mind beyond theirs.

4

Kitty Paddy Brian was on the trot early next day. She had an excuse to poke her head in every door with 'I won't sit. I'm on my way to Nora's,' Nora was Kitty's only sister and she lived in the last house to the South of the island while Kitty's house was one of the most Northern. Kitty was never known to show her face without giving a warning that she was coming; she had a 'made' cough that every woman on the island knew.

There was often a hurried besom, sweeping the floor by the time she darkened the door. Kitty had a habit of noticing something she could praise in or around every house she called at, be it as little as a pullet promising to lay her first egg soon, a thriving calf, a cow nearing her time and making a good show of milk. No, Kitty was not one for tittle tattle; not as far as anybody knew. But a woman with so sharp an eye for what could earn the good word could not but notice things she kept to herself. Or did she? That was the worry. The only house she sat in, and she always shut the door behind her when she crossed that doorstep, was Duffy's. What went on then? Did she empty her mind into Susan Duffy's ear? It was no good to try to fish for a word from Susan but the very idea that two women spread out the island before them and went over it together was a scourge. Not that Susan Duffy was a puzzle in herself, for what she said was within the bounds of things known to them all. If Kitty talked it died with Susan.

Kitty raced in and out of Hughie Duffy's the morning after the seagulls for she took it into her head that Hughie was somehow on trial. The island had been cold to his jail idea. Now they could see what was at the root of it. If they followed him and the grounds around the houseless islands proved empty they could make a jeer of him. Susan took Kitty's chatter lightly. Nobody could make a jeer of Hughie Duffy. When the island was paralysed with fear he got it to its feet. If this did not work out, Hughie would think of something else.

For once in her life Kitty carried something said to her in one house on the tip of her tongue to the next: Susan Duffy was as cocky as a young rooster. She would not hear of failure. And the women who were having second thoughts were far from sure whether what she said lifted their hearts or only proved that Kitty was as near to Susan Duffy as they feared. How much nearer? It looked now that Susan used Kitty as her messenger, for unless bid to talk Kitty never chose to carry Susan's words round with her. No, she would never do it without leave. Still nobody sulked. The men were as cheery as if the herring were in the West bay so the women made gay noises too, a touch of make-believe in their gaiety.

The week passed and the boats came back in a tight cluster; the boat that could shoot ahead of the others trimmed her sails to hold her in check. The Green was crowded when they reached Poolban and clearly they were pleased with themselves. It was a while before sense could be made out of the jumble of shouts. The shelters were up. The two crews caught more lobsters in a week than in a whole season. As for bait fishing, just a shiny hook was enough to cast. It was too late in the season for a second trip that year. There was no shelter for the boats, no inlet, just a wide beach of shingle with restless waves breaking on it. No fewer than ten men were needed to haul a boat out of harm's way.

The noise faded and people emptied on to the footpaths. Kitty made no let-on about carrying one man's talk on to another floor. Going by what Big Jim said Hughie Duffy was like Brian Boru that saved Ireland from the Danes. There were those who said in fun that he would cripple the island with sore bones. Kitty could scarce wait for night for every sore or grumble would be gone over by her fire. And right enough it was a night of talk. Hughie Duffy's idea of boats that could make their way to and back the same day was clearly one that should be used. But there was something else to study: The new fishing grounds should be left to men like Hughie Duffy and Big Jim, men who were rearing families. They checked over six names. Men who had their families reared like Johnny Anthon and Conal Andy and Paddy Brian could keep scraping the grounds within reach. But what about Johnny Anthon and Conal Andy's sons? Would they agree to bide by the home grounds? There were hopes they would be easy led for they might be glad to get out of the hardship of sleeping on straw, even for good reward. Only herring fishing would hold the young. Take that son of Johnny Anthon that had fixed up to marry Annie Neil with his father's blessing and hers. Already he was gurning that he wouldn't put another stone on a stone, and the house up to the windows, and would give the herring only one more year to show up else he and Annie would up and head for Boston. That was how it would be; the island would soon be down to the fry and the spents. Men with weak children had to make do somehow and pray that the herring would be back before their children grew up and scattered or that Hughie Duffy's idea would be heeded. Kitty seated in the recessed bed listened and stored up the best of the talk to hurry with it to Susan next morning.

The island was going to scatter like a barrel that had shed its hoops unless the herring came back. Still it would be hard to blame the young people if they upped and away being free footed. There were people tethered to keep some life on the island. 'Chokin' to you Kitty Paddy Brian, we're not tethered. Childers no burden when they come out of happiness like ours. Hughie would not leave the island, nor would I if we had nothing to hold us but the island itself.'

'Bully on you Susan. That's the kind of talk the island needs for there is grumbling and one that grumbles most is Big Jim's Mary.' 'Mary Jim grumbling? I wouldn't heed her. She and Big Jim's mother is on edge with one another and talk of Boston is only to upset Nora. This island is the pick of the world. You know that yourself Kitty. You were in Boston and you were glad to follow Paddy Brian back when his father died leaving his mother alone, and marry him.' 'I followed Paddy

22

Brian and married him but that's another story. Yon woman will drive poor Nora out of her mind. Still there was a time if talk like this was to be heard I'd have listened for I was restless and I'd be as flighty as Mary Jim; not that I have any time for her. Like I said before it was not her I had in mind.

'Talking of Mary Jim: she is a changed woman. When we were chasing around together she was the butterfly among us; all brooches and beads. I mind her coming to school one day with a necklace of safety pins. And girl grown she could never pass a stall on a fair day without buying a comb or some shiny gee-gaw. Now look at her. She's as near as no matter to being a streel. She should be happy with her four children about her and a fine man like Big Jim to lean on. We were like sisters, Mary Cormac and me.'

'You were like sisters, but not anymore. Be on your guard if you talk to her now for like I said she's as near to being touched as a woman can be this side of The Big House. She has her knife in Nora. She stopped getting her her ounce of twist tobacco. But she gets things for herself any woman could do without. I keep Nora in tobacco and I don't go behind backs to do it. That's when I heard about elastic shillings. Big Jim doesn't know. Nora would not tell him and she made me promise I wouldn't. Nora is ready to thole anything for peace. But there is not much peace in yon house and Nora gets her ear to Mary Jim in a tantrum and then she gets scared. That's when she runs to me. All that's standing in Nora's behalf now is that Mary Jim never knows when I may drop in. I put the fear of God into her once. I pity Big Jim.' 'I pity the two of them,' Susan said quietly.

5

Winter came early that year for, with no fishing, nights were free from early October. Young people made it a wonder winter. They shoaled between the two houses that made them welcome and danced to the music of fiddle, melodeon, flute or maybe as little as the man or woman of the house lilting. The cheery whoop 'mind the dresser' was bugled more often. There was a new gaiety. No one said it but there was an air of a cheery send off in it.

When Spring came young men willingly took to the spade and tilled as much ground as could be spared from grazing. The island was fighting back and one man going by another would greet him with 'people's not seagulls.'

The time came for Summer fishing. The Summer fishing of the new grounds was good but it was drab and far from being as rewarding as the herring. October came but no seagulls. A scribble of snow on the mountains beyond told that Winter was at hand. The scribble of snow and the seagulls went together in people's minds. They made different promises, came at different times and they meant different things but they were truthful. Now, only

24

the snow came, turning the grey peaks white. The snow saddened the island because it told that the days of hope were over.

Another gay winter for the youth. They seemed to grow noisier and jollier and this time made no secret that their dances were farewell affairs, something to look back on later. Early in Spring five of them, three girls and two men would be off. The elders, gathered in Paddy Brian's kitchen, could not blame them. It would be touch and go whether the island would hold together if the herring did not come. Still Boston was a Godsend They had their own before them there. They would be going among neighbours. With nothing new to talk about and tiring of the worn out memories of better days there was more storytelling that Winter than ever before. The first night of storytelling had its own mould. Nobody said straight out 'tell us a story.' There was a set opening. Some bit of news was doubted by Neddy Billy who scratched in his whiskers as he spoke his doubt. 'The way the world is, a body does not know what to believe beyond what he sees with his own two eyes. They talk about Napoleon, John L. Sullivan, Colmcille, Ned Kelly — who knows if the like of them ever was.'

This was Paddy Brian's cue. He seldom spoke but he pushed to the fore now. 'Oh by heavens, Ned Kelly was in it. I met a man in Boston and I had it from his own lips that he saw Ned Kelly and the bullets bouncing off him like hailstones.'

Paddy Brian's story was soon told and following on it there would be a murmur of wonder, held below the level of words so that nothing would be in the way of the next man moved to raise his voice. The second story would rest on direct experience

25

too. It might be something that happened to a man's grandfather and it would have more wonder in it than Paddy Brian's Ned Kelly. There would be a throaty murmur again. The third man would rid his throat and tell of an adventure his uncle heard from a man who spent a lifetime in Australia. It would balloon more and more with wonder. There might be another story and another, the magic growing with each. Then would come the great moment of the night. Hughie Charlie would rid his throat. 'I saw myself coming one night from playing cards . . . . . .' Hughie Charlie's story topped all the others. Nobody ever heard the match of it. As soon as it was told men were free to talk and laugh. They got to their feet and if it was a night that called for the like they lit their lanthorns.

Kitty hurried to Susan's without darkening a door on her way back from her sister's. There was hardship in yon house. Big Jim handed over every penny he earned but yon woman was no house-keeper. She got thro' more sugar and jam than a hotel and all you heard from her is 'a shilling is not made of elastic, you can't get it to stretch.' Susan was the only woman who could do what had to be done; get the women out to earn. There was good money in periwinkles and carrageen moss but no woman among them would show her need by putting on a bag apron and taking to the strand. The world knew there was no shortage in Duffy's of Poolban. No family gets so many fat letters from Boston. Besides Hughie was always a shade luckier than others. If Susan would take to the strand no woman would see any shame in following. Kitty would mind her children for her.

So began the bustle of noisy women scrabbing

for periwinkles and, when the tide suited, picking carrageen moss. They wore old shoes of their husbands but no stockings and the wet hems of their skirts all but drew blood from their raw legs. They made a cheery job of it, and found time to catch razor fish, red crabs and mussels for their own use. The island was doing its best to be gay, in a forced way; Mary Jim worked as hard as anybody and it was near to the end of the season that Susan, plucking carrageen alongside her, heard a wheeze of a tune that sounded like something was dying in her; that tears were only an eyeflick away. She edged Mary away from the others so that she could have a word with her.

Susan spoke quietly but Mary Jim did not whisper back. 'Take your eyes off me, Susan Duffy, and your mind. You're the cause of all this carry on.' And snatching up her wicker basket she sheered away to another flag careless that her skirt trailed in the salt water. Taken aback Susan let on not to hear or heed. She wept silently. A cloud between her and Mary Jim was a heart break. She noticed that other women kept their distance from her. Susan was first back that day. Kitty had an errand to run and hurried away. Susan had only changed her skirt and rubbed her raw legs with vaseline when Mary Jim walked in. Without a word they embraced. Susan was the first to talk. 'It would break my heart, Mary Jim, if you held anything against me. You're right to blame me if blame is the word for bringing the women of the island out among the rocks. But doesn't the island need the few shillings we get from the floating shop for what we pick and pluck?'

'It's not that Susan. It's the island itself. I hate it.

I hate the empty sea around it. When I see us scrabbing like a pack of starlings feeding I want to scream. Am I going out of my mind, Susan?'

'Mary Jim, who likes the slapping of wet skirts against her bare legs? Some nights my legs is afire and it's all I can do not to cry. But the island has to live. Us, women with children around our feet have to strive.'

'I ought never to have married Big Jim. Hadn't I Boston to turn to.'

'You married a good man Mary Cormac and don't forget it. And take care you don't upset him and drive him to the drink with your whining. You have your health and he has his. Count your blessings for a change; and get out of that wet skirt and put on one of mine and sit. I'll make a sup of tea. Do as you're bid for once' she chided with mock severity.

Mary Jim had no sooner gone than Kitty coughed. 'It's a miracle of God you were able to hold yourself to check this long' Susan greeted her. 'What had she to say' Kitty asked, breathless. 'Did she tell you what's eating her?'

'One thing she didn't have to tell is that her mother-in-law has the nosiest sister in the world.'

'I should have known better than to try to pick a word out of you. But I know what I saw. Mary Jim left this house with a lot lighter step than she had going in. And she was wearing a skirt of yours and had her own on her arm.'

'God bless your eyes. They're the best trained eyes on the island.' 'I'll get to the root of what passed between you somehow. But not from you Susan Duffy.' Kitty tightened her headscarf and went out.

6

ohnny Anthon had a busy time. The boyos in Dublin reached out the dole to the countryside. The T.D.'s brother was a County Councillor and his right hand man in keeping the countryside behind him. Johnny Anthon had a trick of his own that worked. He used the birth certificate of a person in Boston to wangle the old age pension for somebody of that name and reasonably within reach of the age. All the proof the pension committee ever needed was the Councillor's word that he saw the man or woman and by their step you would judge them much older than seventy; the bones age people on an island.

When the word came that the dole was to reach out to the islands Johnny Anthon spent a whole day on the mainland and made sure he knew the ins and outs of it all; he would need nobody to teach him the short cuts once he knew the rules, and there was no rule like 'money down', the one that stood between Hughie Duffy and motor boats. The island heard with wonder of the blessings within their reach. Conal Andy and Paddy Brian praised Johnny Anthon for what he did. The only stumble taken out of him was when Hughie Duffy asked him would any young man on the island build a house because of this money. 'I'll tell you what it puts me in mind of — the jail on the day when the shout was raised 'parcels up.' To be sure the parcels were a Godsend. When we had our feed we were still in jail!' But Hughie took what was going like anybody else.

There were still cases of want that Johnny Anthon couldn't bring within the rules. Mary Brian was one, so he started a cry that the island needed a post office and he got every householder on the island to sign a petition. The T.D. made a great to-do about the trouble he had in getting Dublin to listen to him. But Mary Brian got the Post Office for, tho' her name was not on anybody's tongue, everybody knew what was in Johnny Anthon's mind from the start.

Ellen Ferry was a trickier case. Ellen was in with a woman who was only cousin to her and it would warm her seat at that fireside if a few shillings came in through her. Ellen was a frail poor body and even scrabbing among the rocks was beyond her. There was nobody of her name in Boston nearing seventy. Ellen herself was only forty. It was Conal Andy that gave Johnny the line to take on Ellen's case. Ellen could make neither head nor tail of colours. Ellen should get the blind pension. This was beyond the County Councillor so his brother the T.D. came in to prove he was always within reach and put it to Johnny Anthon's good sense that nothing could be done for Ellen. The plain fact was she wasn't blind and the pension was for blind people. Again it was Conal Andy who played the winning card. Ellen Ferry was as near to being blind as the doctor's wife's brother was to being the man the T.D.'s brother made him out to be when his name came up before the County Council for a rate collector.

That shook the T.D. and he made his big mistake. 'Look, suppose I get the doctor to sign the papers and then an inspector comes round where would he be?' Johnny Anthon had the answer to that on the tip of his tongue. He knew a woman they could borrow. She was blind as a bat and healthy as a trout.

The T.D. got angry. It was the last time he would do anything for Johnny Anthon. He strode away, anger on his heels. He hung on the step long enough to say back over his shoulder: 'Ellen Ferry will get her blind pension and may God forgive me.' 'You'll have the prayers of the island' Johnny Anthon told him.

As soon as the T.D. went out of sight the Three Wise Men took out their pipes. That was sign enough. Johnny Anthon raised his head when people near him would cheer. The T.D. was still within hearing. He might feel himself mocked.

By Johnny Anthon's measurement no house was now in want. The country never had such a government; what with this new money, the women's earnings and the good catches in the new fishing grounds the island could withstand the loss of the herring. True, no young person would trust himself to it and settle down on the island. There was sense in Hughie Duffy's talk about big boats but there was no use in harping on it. They had it from the T.D. himself that a ring of foreign fishing boats broke up the shoals before even they could reach the island. A man with money for a down payment was what the island needed to get its share.

Johnny Anthon never looked beyond the plight of

a neighbour and there was nobody he did not ease things for in some way except Minnie MacBride. She was the only householder he could not wangle on to the dole. The whole island knew how things were with Minnie MacBride. Neighbours had special reasons for worrying about her. She lived alone and she with bones that no more than let her crawl around her kitchen and stumble to the hen house to gather eggs. People were at one that there was sense in her sister Bella's idea that she should go to live with her on the mainland; Bella was married to a stonemason on the mainland with a few acres across the bay. But they had to pick their words even with Bella for fear a word would drift back and maybe sound like the island was tired of doing chores for her. So they pooh-poohed any talk Bella tried to link them with that could hurt Minnie if it got back to her and maybe make her give in to Bella and she still in a swither. Is it trouble to us you would make her out to be? Well indeed she is no such thing. All we do for her when all is said and done is to see that there is a full creel of turf at the weather door at nightfall, a bucket of spring well water on the block of wood by the dresser and that the doors to her hen and duck houses are shut; children's work, all of it. And they made light, too, of the few jobs that fell on the men of the island: What were they but to cut her turf every April and by the same token she had the best bank of turf on the island. That only meant three men for one day. Every third year her house had to be thatched and roped so that she need have no worry on a stormy night. And there was no let-on in their talk for this was the island's way; its nature. At the same time a body had but to see Minnie on the hearth with the tongs in her hands and her big, lazy lump of a dog stretched out in front of the ashes to dread what would happen if she stumbled. And that was where Bella's talk found an echo on the island. Minnie would be safe with Bella. But would she be happy? As she was, she wanted for nothing for she was not left make-do with the price she got for her eggs. Her two brothers in Boston sent her money every Christmas. Indeed, only for her bones she would be the most at her ease of all the women of her age on the island. It was a heart scald that there was nobody of the right age of her name in Boston for then she would no longer look on herself as a burden on Bella. It would be a poor thing for a woman to join a thronged fireside with nothing coming into it through her. Minnie did not hide her mind from her neighbours: Bella was good natured and her man was kindly but it would take only one grumble and that maybe only half meant to turn the bite a body ate into ashes in her mouth. And once she went out from the island there would be no coming back. 'In God's name, unless the island is tired of me . . . . .' And the island was quick to cry out against such talk. Minnie had her own warm house with its floor to herself and they had no wish to see her go. Here again there was no put-on for they knew of a woman who went out from the island to live with her daughter on the mainland who came to rue the day she left her own fireside. If that could happen to a woman who went to live with her daughter was it not more risky to go into a house where the other woman was only a sister? As against that maybe two sisters would make a better fist of living together, for grandmothers could not help taking a hand in the rearing of their grandchildren. There would be little danger of the like with Minnie, and anyway look at how the children of the island liked doing things for her.

Still while there was a doubt in Minnie's mind she would stay where she was. If her bones got any worse there would be nothing for her but to go to Bella. Maybe somebody should say to her to get rid of that dog, but then who would she have to talk to? It was all a bit of a puzzle.

Minnie MacBride's house — the word cottage was not known on the island — was in a hollow by an inlet that was a handy landing place for two neighbour men who fished lobsters. They had cause to go to their boats a couple of times a day and one or other was sure to walk in on Minnie's floor to light his pipe. He would notice the level of turf in the creel and water in the bucket and as like as not he would put down a new fire.

Minnie was rarely seen outside although she often rested her arms on the half door. She was a comely woman and those who knew her before her bones went back on her said that she was as free striding a girl as was on the island. And another thing: The touch of show off she had in her as a girl was still with her. Notice the way she dressed herself, and throw an eye at her dresser; as shiny as was on the island. She made no moan over herself. Bella had the right of things on her side but there was sense too, in what Minnie said. If a mistake had to be made let the island have no hand act or part in it.

One day when it was Kitty Paddy Brian's turn to take Minnie's gathering of eggs for the week to the floating shop talk which began as quiet wonder at how well her hens and ducks were laying roused itself into a full scale talk on Minnie herself and the way that was on her. The T.D. himself was there that day. He asked this and that about Minnie and then said there was a way out for her that would let her walk in, head up, on Bella's floor. He knew of people willing to pay good money for a site to build a house on the island, especially an island that was easy to get at, and with the price he could get her for her land in her fist Minnie would not feel herself a burden anywhere.

On a Tuesday the crews made excuses to fore-gather on The Green where the woman on their way home from the floating shop doled out the weekly ration of tobacco. This day they brought more. The T.D.'s promise that he would get people to pay Minnie MacBride a lapful of money for her place was mocked at by everybody except Johnny Anthon. Look at how strangers were making Summer homes for themselves by the sea outside: one of them was bound to raise his eyes to the island, and don't forget that T.D. made an auction-eer of himself. He would know. Conal Andy led the scoffers and in the end the women's story was beat-en down. Still, on their way home, they went back to it for it was a joy to have something to talk of besides the well-worn gossip of the island. It was all very well for Conal Andy to mock the idea that a stranger would think of buying his way onto the island. But . . . . .

And their eyes were watchful next morning and the time came to shout one to the other that the T.D.'s boat was on its way. There were two strangers in the boat. Something was afoot. Women raised their voices to ask one another should they hurry down to Minnie's. In the end they clustered in the

35

kitchen of the house nearest to it. As soon as the T.D. and the two strangers went into Minnie's they spilled down to the boat to pick what news they could out of the crew. And the crew were forthcoming: From what they overheard it looked that what these island people had in mind was a summer house for themselves on the island. Who or what they were the crew did not know beyond that they were not Irish nor English nor Scots nor Yankee. They kind of crumbled their words down in their throats as they spoke.

The women withdrew when the T.D. and The Strangers came out again. As the boat pushed off they raced to Minnie's. 'What under God is afoot?' Minnie had a story to tell: she was at the half door when the boat landed. She knew the T.D. by sight and she nearly dropped dead when she saw him with two people she never saw before on his heels making for her door. She had to quieten the dog for any footstep he never heard before always upset him. She barely had that done when the T.D. walked in on the floor. The other two kind of held back at first. 'Like I said I'm here to get you a lapful of money for your house and your bit of land.' He spoke in Gaelic. The other two crossed the doorstep and they said something to one another and it was not in any tongue Minnie ever heard. It looked to her that they were not too pleased with the T.D. for having a word with her over their heads. 'Ask her what her price is,' said the woman. Minnie judged the pair of them to be man and wife. She wouldn't know what to make of it all only for a whisper she got from Kitty, so she said to herself, 'go easy Minnie.' She let on she wasn't sure she wanted to leave the island at all unless she got a

36

price that tempted her. There was a gurgle of praise
from the women. Then up spoke the man to say to
the T.D. that he hadn't come to bargain. 'Just tell
her what my first and last word is.' So the T.D. said
to Minnie that he could get her five hundred pounds
and that it was a good price and that she should
jump at it. Minnie was so taken aback she did not
know what to say. To give herself a chance to get
her wits together she said that she would have to
talk it over with her sister Bella and he said he
would have Bella and her man in the next morning
and that his boat would land at Poolban so that the
whole island would know what was afoot and have
a say in it.

There was the whole story. Story? A Miracle.
The island would now have something worth talking
about. Something live, not worn out topics beaten
flat from overuse: How are ye all over there this
morning: is it true your cow calved — a fine young
heifer calf: and whisper me this — many a thing has
to be whispered on an island.

37

7

Next morning there was a lot of make-believe in and out of byres by women. Men on The Green, too, raised heads without cause for a stolen look at the shore beyond. Conal Andy kept his eyes on his work of darning meshes into a torn net, but the moving heads did not go without notice. He mocked at the idea that the T.D.'s boat would show up. Johnny Anthon, baiting a long line, sat with his back to the mainland but he spoke over his shoulder to Paddy Brian that Conal Andy, as always, had the wrong end of the story; Conal Andy never rightly studies anything. Yesterday's talk made too much sense to fall apart. Bella would come: there would be a penny in this for the T.D. and he wasn't one to miss that.

A woman standing to look around her between byre and kitchen door was the first to spot the brown jib with the white patch. Her shout drew men's eyes towards the houses and what they saw made them straighten their backs and stare, — women dashing on to the footpaths. They, at least, believed in yesterday's talk and were ready. Men knew before they turned their heads mainland-

38

wards that the T.D.'s boat was in sight.

The noisiest among the hurrying women was Kitty Paddy Brian. Was not all this her doing? There was time for banter for though the breeze was fresh it was a shade bare for Poolban. When the T.D.'s boat put about it was clear that there were five people aboard. The T.D. himself sat on the aft thwart; it was easy to pick him out by his headgear. But there was a woman in the boat? If Bella was not there what meaning could there be in this sudden rush back to the island? The steam went out of the noise. It was Conal Andy gave the growing throng of women new hope. When did anybody ever see Bella but in a man's jacket? And yonder she was on the tiller; no better hand on a tiller than the same Bella.

Kitty Paddy Brian could raise her voice to boast again. Only that she started the talk at the floating shop Minnie would still be stuck to her fireside without a glint of hope.

Then a strange thing happened. All of a sudden Mary Jim shouted her way to the front. She whipped off her apron, careless who saw the stains on it, and cheered like mad, leaping up and down. Her voice had a musical bugle to it that maybe she didn't know of herself, or notice now when it rang out for the first time. Her shout reached Bella and she got to her feet and shouted a hello back. She grabbed the T.D.'s Tam O'Shanter and waved. This was met by a confusion of fluttering aprons for it was enough to show that Bella and the T.D. were on the same word. Mary Jim headed the gust of women to the flat flag that was the landing place. Kitty was in the throng but she no longer headed the pack. The T.D. sat on. His share of the work was done. Now was the turn of the island. There was a short stay on The Green for hand-shakes and greetings but Mary Jim was in a hurry and nobody was far from sharing her fever. The quicker they got to Minnie the better. If there was still any swither in her, now was the time to brush it aside. But it was only women who had a share in that job. They were the ones to deal with Minnie. The men strayed off to their boats for it was time to make the rounds.

Kitty, sulking a little, was no longer breaking her toes with hurry. She took time for a word with Susan Duffy; Susan was one of the young women tethered to her own floor by young children. But a new shout from those on their way to Minnie's was too much for Kitty. She hopped up on a rock and shaded her eyes with her hands. 'Will you for heaven's sake look — Minnie MacBride out at her own gable. Something not seen for years. I'm off, Susan, but I'll be back under full sail and I'll give you every last word of the story.' She spoke over her shoulder for she was already on her way.

And back she was, a panting Kitty, with a wonder-tale. 'Hold your tongue, Susan, we were all wrong about Minnie. She was only waiting for the wind of a word from us to be off with Bella. I picked that up from something she let slip; thanking God we held her back long enough for this fortune to come her way. Listen to me: Some of yon noise was not because of Minnie. There were women in that crowd saying to themselves that if Minnie MacBride could get five hundred pounds, their places would fetch more.'

'Don't be daft, Kitty.' Susan pushed a chair forward for Kitty but she was in no mood to sit.

She would have to race around among the houses with her ear cocked to find out if anybody saw the meaning as herself in the noise at Minnie's. Somebody was sure to talk about Mary Jim, and how she was fair leaping out of her skin. 'Mark my words, Susan, we have a changed Mary Jim on our hands.'

'I'm glad to hear it. Anything that lifts her back to her old self is to be welcomed. She used to be the tearaway of the island. What harm if she says to herself that Big Jim's place is worth double what Minnie got? It will do her good.'

Kitty listened patiently. 'You know Mary Jim surely Susan, but I saw her growing up too and I'm not blind. I'm saying no word against her. She is married to Big Jim, my sister's son, as good natured a man as ever sat on an oar. But I saw what I saw and I heard what I heard and maybe I know things you don't know, smart and all as you are.'

'Go on Kitty' Susan mocked. 'No girl would be good enough for Big Jim in your eyes.'

'One thing sure is that it wasn't Mary Cormac I had in my mind nor in my prayers.' There was less bounce in her step going down the floor. At the doorstep she paused. 'Bear in mind that this is the first time ever on this island the mainland touched us and now it lets loose the idea of how much money any place is worth. There are people on the island could get strange notions. There is no telling what will come of all this.'

Kitty had already gone out of sight past the corner of the gable by the time Susan got to the open door. Just then the first crew back from the fishing ground came into view. Susan withdrew into the shadow of the kitchen and watched. There were two men with a pocket net slung between them.

41

Instead of spreading it out to dry, and freeing it from crabs and dog fish, they simply flung it down in a heap and walked off. Other crews came in and they too hurried home without a stop for either a smoke or a chat. Men were in as much a rush for news of what happened at Minnie's as the women but they tried to hide it and what they heard lost nothing in the telling. The more it was spoken of the greater grew the wonder of it. A detail in nearly every telling was the carry on of Mary Jim. Men took her lightly. There were people on the island who would make a wonder out of the chirping of a cricket. Mary Jim was always a shade feather headed. A day would come when she would be herself again.

8

Bella stayed on with Minnie to get her things together for her journey to the mainland. There was no reason why she should not set out at once for her new fireside. Any odds and ends of things outstanding to give over her house and land to The Strangers could as well be done outside; easier. Bella talked Minnie out of taking too much truck with her but whatever else Minnie was willing to let go of she would not hear of leaving her hens or ducks or dog behind. Bella tried hard to make a stand about the dog but in the end it was simply no dog no sale.

Minnie's going kept the firesides in talk. The day she left was as much an affair of the whole island as if she was somebody heading for Boston. With a shoulder to lean on she hobbled to the boat. She was lifted in. She wept and there were few dry eyed women among the throng of neighbours waving to her until the boat went out of sight around the point. Before draining off over the footpaths there was gloomy talk that she would wither away thinking long after the island. And then there was her house. Minnie would worry about that too for it did not take an empty house long to lose its looks.

The first sign of drab would be soot marks on the gable. Bella should have left word with somebody to light at least one fire every day. To be sure there was no lock on the door and a body could go in and put down a fire but unless Minnie herself or the T.D. gave the word the best thing might be to leave the next step to The Strangers themselves. Anyway it would be wise to wait until the day of the floating shop. The T.D. might have a word to say then.

But there was no need to wait, for bright and early next morning while the men were still gathering on The Green the T.D.'s boat, low down in the water with cargo, put out from the shore beyond: the red gunwale might not show up as quick as the white patched jib but it told the same story. There was sense in the rowing for the ebb tide would be a help and anyway there was scarce a breath of wind. Besides the crew there were two men, but it was not the crew nor the strange men The Green puzzled over but the cargo. Long sighted Conal Andy was the first to make out part of it. There was timber and, it would be his guess, cement. The timber and the cement was a guide who the extra men might be — carpenters, and they were men that did many an odd job on the island. So The Strangers were no dozers. They knew it was not wise to let a house get cold. Going by the cargo it looked that they had in mind to make it a place to live in; as like as not they would build another house nearby later on. The carpenters were neighbourly men, but one of them was a great man for tales of the Fianna. Their coming would brighten the evenings at Paddy Brian's fireside. As well as that they would give the whole story behind their coming and more besides for they would have the news of the countryside, and there were no knots on their tongues. Kitty Paddy Brian was within earshot of the talk on The Green. When the men moved off to their boats she turned to Susan. Just then a new sound rattled along the shore. It was the drumming of a motor. Men, halfway to their boats, paused to look. They left it to Conal Andy of the searching eyes to pick out what he could, how many people were in the motor boat? Kitty moved close to listen.

Conal Andy made out that The Strangers at least were aboard — the man stranger was on the tiller. The T.D. sat in the stern with him. The woman was in the bows. And the two boats were on the same errand for when the motor boat came alongside the engine died and the oars idled. Then both began moving again. They were on their way to Minnie's: What else.

Well, whatever was afoot there was no need to miss the morning's round over it. It would be all gone over by Paddy Brian's blazing fire come nightfall.

But Kitty Paddy Brian was not willing to wait for the carpenters to tell the story. She dodged through the rocks and she saw what was to see, a thing such as had never come the island's way before. The motor boat was first to the inlet. It cut power and circled around until it lost speed. The cargo boat came alongside. There was a lobster boat in Minnie's inlet with a man sitting on a thwart having a quiet smoke. The woman in the motor boat called to him and used her hand to show that she wanted him out of the way. He looked this side and that and Kitty could see his mind at work and indeed it was her own idea too. There was room enough for the other boats to go by. But the woman shouted again and there was even a hint of anger in the way she moved her hand this time. In no good humour — Kitty could judge that by the way he dipped his oar in the water — the man in the lobster boat sculled out. Then the other two moved in.

Conal Andy was right. The cargo was mostly timber and bags of cement. The carpenters and the crew piled everything on the grass in front of Minnie's. The T.D. and The Strangers walked around, pointed here and there and then studied a big sheet of paper. Kitty dare not risk going close enough to catch a word they said. When the cargo was laid out the motor boat left the inlet and the other boat followed. The rest of the story was everybody's, for women, who had clustered by gables close by, spilled down to get it from the carpenters. What Kitty saw was enough to run with while it was fresh. Let the rest come later.

The carpenters were open about their errand. So far as they knew, The Strangers had plans to fix up Minnie's house and make do with it for a while. There was little to wonder at in that, but a wonder did come that startled the island. The Strangers had rules to bar any boat from Minnie's inlet and to deny the right to use any path over the land. To make this double clear the carpenters were to nail up a board with the words printed on it and they were words the island never heard before. *No Trespass.* The carpenters knew what they meant. It was simple enough: No boat in the inlet: No foot on Minnie's land.

Kitty felt cheated on her way back from her

46

rounds to find that this new wave of news had swept past her. All she could do was hurry to Susan's. What was the world coming to? The Strangers must have the temper of cross dogs. What would Hughie Duffy say when he got back come Saturday?

The women of the island made a lot of angry noise about *No Trespass;* it was a Godsend to get something they could tear to pieces and not tramp on anybody's toes.

Conal Andy too spoke out against No Trespass and roused others so much that they were for throwing it to the tide. 'Do nothing until Hughie Duffy gets home' Johnny Anthon pleaded. It was the first time he felt his word needed backing. Even Conal Andy gave in to wait Hughie's word.

Johnny Anthon may not have noticed power shifting itself to Hughie Duffy and anyway he would not have grudged it. He could see sense in what Conal Andy would have done if he had his way. It would be easy to throw *No Trespass* to the tide, and that was where it belonged. The carpenters would not stand in their way nor name anybody doing it. They were neighbourly men. There was one thing they could not do however, hide what happened 'No Trespass' from The Strangers. And what would they do? They would tell the guards who would be in asking this and that. Well the island could sing dumb. It was good at that, but the guards had eyes in their heads. Could they help noticing that every house had a dog and fine they would know there was not as much as one dog licence on the island. And what about that pile of timber at Conal Andy's gable? The island knew how it came the guards would come and there would be trouble. To be sure *No Trespass* was bad manners. Conal Andy had the right of that but the island had to study other things. And when all was said and done what about the inlet of Minnie's? It was only a fair-weather landing place while a man had a meal. It would be no great hardship to lose the use of it. And as for the paths over Minnie MacBride's land they were no loss either. Nobody would have an errand that way. Maybe the right thing to do was to talk to the T.D. He knew these people. When Hughie Duffy landed Conal Andy and Johnny Anthon both put their cases to him. 'I think you'd best be said by Johnny Anthon.' He chuckled and went on his way.

And by chance the young people that night gave *No Trespass* its place in the life of the island. In the midst of their zestful dancing a girl whooped out 'No Trespass' and behold it took the place of 'Mind the dresser.' It became a joke, and once the island got a grip on the word it used it as a greeting. Even Kitty Paddy Brian on her rounds changed from Dia Annso to *No Trespass*.

9

The island had no rule about sending their children to bed early but they had such wide spaces for play that sleep came early. Susan and Hughie spent a while by the last fire of the night, Susan in the corner with her darning or patching or knitting and Hughie with his bedtime pipe. Susan often let her fingers idle while she watched him fill it, for like everything on the island filling a pipe had a pattern of its own. Hughie took out his plug of tobacco and cut wafers into the palm of his left hand. With a pipeful cut he put the plug away, but the penknife remained open in his right hand. It was held between the thumb and first finger blade up. With the heel of his right hand he pulped the tobacco in his left palm. When this was done he brought the knife into use again to poke out the leftover in his pipe from the earlier smoke. This was guided to rest on top of the new tobacco. Not until this was done did he shut his penknife and put it away. He set the bowl of the pipe against the heel of his left hand in such a way that the scorched leftover was last into it. He pressed gently with his thumb and then reached for the tongs and took a coal out of the fire. Susan mocked that a woman never took more care mixing a cake. 'I be watching you, waiting for you to waggle your fingers to make sure no dust of tobacco goes to waste. You even poke the little finger of your right hand between the fingers of your left to make double sure you get it all.' 'Filling a pipe is half a smoke in itself. The man that can't fill a pipe should never smoke.' 'It's a joy to see a man light a new filled pipe. Now and then I wish I had a bit of tobacco to give Johnny Anthon for half the time the pipe is dead in his mouth" 'Honest to God, Susan, you are a bit daft. Johnny Anthon and Conal Andy and Paddy Brian can get round you — giving in to let them have our good lamp every Sunday night this Winter for their card playing.' He chuckled as he said it. She made a face at him. 'What else could I do man with poor Conal Andy playing the five of hearts on his partner's Jack thinking it the five of diamonds and all because of that old smokey lamp that Kitty Paddy Brian keeps?' She frowned in thought. 'I sometimes think, Hughie that the island doesn't half thank Johnny Anthon for all he does. The way that man keeps in mind the ages of people in Boston to see no birth certificate goes to loss is nothing short of a miracle.' Hughie puffed for a moment. He took the pipe from his mouth. 'When you are bait fishing, Susan, you throw out scraps of food to draw fish around your hook. That's what this T.D. of ours does. I suppose that's all the poor fellow is let do to hold votes. He likely sees through Johnny Anthon's tricks; not that they would upset him so long as Johnny Anthon's talk gets him votes.' 'Sometimes I wonder Hughie, if you are not too hard on him. To be fair to him he never met the kind of people you met. Your mind shot past his. He was never in jail. He looks out at the world from inside the counter of a small shop. What you ask of him is beyond his reach. What Johnny Anthon puts to him is within it.' They were both silent for a moment. She laughed softly. 'He can't but know that the birth certificates Johnny Anthon gives him belong to other people.' 'To be sure he knows, but as long as the story carries a skin he will go along with it. He thinks it makes a great fellow of him, the smart man. When we were behind the barbed wire there was a guard who would sometimes flick a piece of tobacco across to us. When he went home on holidays he boasted about it.' He smoked. Susan sat with her hands in her lap. 'Now the barbed wire is this rule they have against us in Dublin to keep us trapped in our hardship. The last thing we had in our minds was that there was any among us could make a rule like that. To be sure the dole is as worthwhile as anything else is but it is only scraps through the wire to keep us quiet.' 'Take care you don't turn yourself against the island Hughie.' He took the pipe from his mouth and fondled the warm bowl. 'Wild horses wouldn't drag me off this island girl and one day we'll get the boats we need. Isn't that why we make a prisoner of every penny we get from Boston?'

'And that's why you make friends with the Scottish crews.' 'I not only put away every penny from Boston but add to it.' She sighed. 'Sometimes I wish you lived all your days here with the rest of us. Your while in jail put you too far ahead. You were changed when you came back. I was afraid of you myself for a while.' 'You weren't the only one' he chuckled. 'I had to sniff the wind, too, in case

51

you had changed. I used to worry about you in jail. Many a night I lay awake.' She shook her head. 'You never wrote to me. I waited and waited. I even prayed, but you never wrote.' 'How could I write, woman, knowing every letter was read before it was let go.' He sat for a moment with the pipe in his hand, frowning in thought. 'Maybe that wasn't the real reason. I was never sure of my spelling. The spelling holds many a man from writing.' He had to relight his pipe. Susan took up her knitting. 'Did I ever tell you that I made up my mind to marry you the day I pulled you by the black head ashore at Poolban? You must have been all of ten years of age at the time. Big Jim was only a stroke or two behind me. I suppose if he had been the one to save you I would have had to let him get you.' She laughed a throaty gurgle. 'I was eleven and I had my eye on you before that but I was afraid Mary Cormac would get inside me. She had a bracelet. Big Jim and you, Mary and me. always the four of us running round together.' She rested her hands in her lap again and there was a moment of silence. Hughie smoked. 'Mary Jim worries me, Hughie. She is not herself.' Hughie was silent. Susan raised her hands and counted stitches. 'You don't put much heed in Kitty Paddy Brian's talk about Mary Jim wondering what Big Jim could get for his place?' Hughie struck the bowl of his pipe against his palm to free the tobacco but he did not speak. 'Tell me something, Hughie, did the men make no fuss about the money Minnie MacBride got?' 'What fuss would we make? Johnny Anthon said all there was to be said: we were glad she got this way out.' He put the pipe back in his mouth and puffed. 'I wish to God the herring would come;

Susan prayed. 'Mary Jim would be as noisy as the rest of us. That's the one thing would rouse the hearts of the women of this island, the herring. It would take the island's mind back to itself. There's scarce a word of island talk since the mainland reached out to Minnie MacBride.'

10

It was maybe because *No Trespass* had become a thing without meaning, that Kitty spoke of it to the T.D. no doubt expecting him to make light of it too. All she said was that this was a queer class of people to put in among them who put up such a sign. But the T.D. flew into a rage. He ranted and raved at everybody for making a wonder of a thing you would see every couple of miles of the road outside. It was the way people lived away out of here — every family shut into itself and minding its own business. He knew people in Dublin who could not name the family six doors away from them, and the houses all put gable to gable. This noise better stop for who knew what day somebody would want him to work the same miracle he wrought for Minnie MacBride? Let a whisper get out much less a shout against *No Trespass* and people with money might cast their eyes somewhere else.

Kitty wanted to tell him it was all in fun she spoke but before she could get her say said Mary Jim turned on her. Why couldn't Kitty hold her tongue? No other woman put a word but they winked at one another when it was safe. They thought they could see through the T.D.'s anger. He was only letting off steam because of the way his arm was twisted over Ellen Ferry. But what was a body to make of Mary Jim? She must have something in her nose for Kitty. Well, if she had, between them be it. Least said soonest mended. Women gathered up their parcels and sauntered off home. It wasn't easy to talk about Mary Jim for she was sib to half the island. A woman would have to look around her and lower her voice before talking of her, but the T.D. was something else. Everybody could laugh at him. He was just a man with a sore toe. Johnny Anthon had best keep away from him.

Kitty kept on Susan's heels on the way back from the boat and followed her in. 'What do you make of Mary Jim now?' 'Never mind about Mary Jim Kitty. What in the world drove you to make out that anybody cares about *No Trespass* anymore? The T.D. thought that you were casting something up at him, hinting that he brought cross dogs in among us.' 'Ach the T.D. I'm not talking about him and well you know it. But this other woman, I'm telling you I had to grind my teeth to keep my tongue quiet.' Kitty went to the door and pushed it shut. There was something she would not breathe to a soul but Susan. Mary Jim was not above sending Big Jim's mother to her for the loan of as much as ten shillings at a time. But Susan did not let her get far with that kind of talk. What harm if Mary Jim went to her for the loan of ten shillings? Wasn't it the same as borrowing an egg to make up the dozen as many a woman did? Didn't the world know that Paddy Brian got a lump of money when his brother was killed in Boston? And there was more: Mary Jim could have worries nobody knew of. She was not looking well. Kitty should mind her tongue . . . And Kitty in no good humour headed for home.

Before the week was out the island saw the T.D. had another cause for his bad humour the day Kitty spoke to him. A mainland woman sent in a paper with a passing boat and there, bold as brass, was a picture of *No Trespass*. How it happened nobody knew; maybe a mainland boat going by took a picture and some busybody sent it to Dublin. But that wasn't the worst of it. By what was written in the newspaper you would think half the island was fenced off and that the people were up in arms against it. Kitty got her hands on the paper and she went from house to house with it, and by the time she came back to Susan she had a whole litany of what this person said and what that person said and she went over it word by word. Hughie happened to be home when she came in with her heated tidings and he only laughed, lit his pipe, and went out. Susan had to give in there was no truth in what was written and agree that it was a shame to raise the island's name in this way.

With Hughie silent, Johnny Anthon had to hold a session on The Green. And for once the men were not left in peace to settle the matter among themselves. Mary Jim, her feathers as ruffled as at the floating shop, with a group of women around her, had a word to say. She was for a boat load of people going out at once to the T.D. to ask him to tell the Strangers that the island had no hand in this and that nobody from the island took the picture. The Strangers should be told the truth. Peace was what they wanted and peace they would get, and so would everybody else that bought land on the island. But Johnny Anthon would not be rushed into anything. Like enough he was in no hurry to face the T.D. Anyway he could see no sense in people upsetting themselves over a story in a paper. The carpenters would know the truth of this and they would laugh at it and they would tell The Strangers to laugh at it. And like enough by now this was an old story to them. The carpenters were by themselves beyond there at Minnie's and he would go across and have a word with them. The way to kill a rumour was to make light of it.

But while Johnny Anthon put a good face on things before the women he was peeved at the use of the island's name in such a way. It was a blessing when night came and the elders took the case under review. Neddy Billy scratching as usual in his whiskers when he spoke, called them all to witness the truth of his words that you could never trust what you read. Let fools believe what they read the island would bide by what it saw or heard. This would be a seven days' wonder if they let it lie. Johnny Anthon had the right of it. The quiet way was the island way. This put him in mind . . . . . He did his best to move the kitchen to stories to get away from the worry of this happening and he got help, but the murmur was not long kept below the level of words. It was welcome news when they heard that so many young people were making a joke of it all. For once the youngsters had the right sense of a thing.

But the quiet way of the island was put in jeopardy. Three boys and two girls landed at Poolban from a hired boat. They looked innocent enough. Likely this was a party going from island to island. But when they began to land no end of gear — if packs and bundles and a couple of light poles could be called gear — the men on The

Green were puzzled and they wondered still more when the youths asked if they could set up their tents on the edge of The Green out of the way of the nets. To be sure they could but wasn't it a bit late in the year for holidays?

The men on The Green had an eye for the skill with knots in the young people's fingers. Nobody asked them straight out why they chose that island and that time of year for their visit, and they were glad when they saw Kitty coming round Hughie's gable. Kitty would soon pick out of them whatever it was they had in mind. Anyway it was time for men to go out the bay. Children came up shyly and were taken notice of. Kitty set to work and it was no easy job to learn much. No, they were not from around here. No, they had not come to learn Irish. Yes, they did come from Dublin. No, they were not working there; they were students. Kitty shied away at that. She knew of a man who came to an island and wrote a book about it and as much as his life would be worth would be to show his face there again. There was no telling what students would say or write. Besides this was a scrap of news in itself worth spreading. Kitty hurried to Susan. 'I declare to God all they need is a tin can or two and they would pass for tinkers.' They were after something. What would students be trying to ferret out on that island? Could it be that these were the same laddie bucks behind the story in the paper? It was up to everybody to keep a guard on her tongue. But Susan had a washing on her hands, and Kitty was not pleased at the easy way she let this news in one ear and out the other. She would go where she would get a better hearing. 'They'll be into you, Susan, or I'll miss my guess. Not indeed that they'll get much out of you.'

Susan had the tongs in her hands at the hearth when there was a gentle tap at the open door. There was a shadow, a person, a girl. Now nobody on the island ever tapped on an open door nor, for that matter, on a closed one; you just raised the latch or pulled the cord and walked in. The girl took a cautious step across the doorstep and spoke. She was sorry to cause trouble but could she boil a kettle? 'God bless us child don't you know you can boil a kettle and never knock on a door, walk straight in. There's spring well water in a bucket at the end of the table. The kettle is here by the fire and there will be a good blaze in a minute.' She hunkered down and fanned the fire with her apron. The girl filled the kettle. 'You have the island dizzy,' Susan chuckled. 'If you are only on a ramble through the island keep it to yourselves. Leave us guessing and there's no telling what we'll make you out to be. And another thing, don't for the life of you say it if you are going to write something or there will be holy murder.'

The kettle boiled and Susan got the teapot ready. 'Call the others in and let you have your meal here at the heat.' Susan was not as free of curiosity as she was letting on.

The girl went to the door and the others came in. One of the young men, and he didn't look the oldest, was open about their errand. It was about this thing, *No Trespass*. There was a plague of these notices and if a stop was not put to them the whole coast would soon be taken over by people with money. There were flying columns of young people like themselves, here there and everywhere, rousing the country to the danger. This was the first time the like of it showed up on an island. The whole country would be watching to see what happened. Susan was at a loss what to say. She was slow to tell them they would not get much of a hearing. For one thing they were too young. What would Johnny Anthon make of youngsters taking it upon themselves to tell grown up men what to do? The only hope for them would be in Hughie. It could put him in mind of the young people he followed long ago. But then those others were known; breed, and seed. These young people came in off the wind.

The youngsters were watching her. She knew they were watching her and that they were making her a test of what to expect. Likely they knew about Hughie. What could she say to them? It wouldn't be fair to give them false hope. Should she tell them that the island looked on *No Trespass* as a joke? And that the story in the paper only made the island angry, or should she leave it to Hughie to have a word with them? She ran her eyes over the eager faces and shook her head. 'I'd be afraid of my life you won't get much of a hearing. The island is mostly said and led by Johnny Anthon and in his eyes you'll be only children. But you will have your say. My man will see to that.' She smiled at the girl who was first in. 'I could give you two girls a bed in the room with the children, the boys could sleep in the loft. Wouldn't you be better off that way than in a tent?' 'We would love it' the girls said eagerly. One of them turned to the boys: 'Maybe that's the way to do it, to let the people get to know us.' But the spokesman for the group wouldn't hear of it. No people would let themselves be fenced off if they knew they could get help. What he wanted was a meeting. Maybe there was a barn on the island; it was not likely they would get the schoolhouse. 'You can gather it here on this floor. People will come to listen to you in this house, so you will be sure of a hearing only don't raise your hopes too high. People will come but they could make fun of you. I will send out word.' After further talk the students withdrew.

They were no more than gone when Kitty came in. She was in such a hurry she all but tripped on the doorstep. There was holy murder going on. One of the children picked up a word and it went round. The students were on the island to make war against *No Trespass* and Mary Jim was not the only one making noise this time. There was no make-believe about the backing she had now. She was a changed woman from the time she used to be mousing around without a word to throw to a dog. Honest to God you would swear she was even bulkier within her clothes. She was like a mad woman. All that was out of her was that the tents should be burned. Somebody should warn these young people outside to make for the mainland before Mary Jim came down on them with the women and children of the island at her back.

'Go out on The Green, Kitty,' Susan urged. 'I see most of the men are back. Johnny Anthon is there. Thank God I hear Hughie whistling. Tell him I said he is to come in. Tell all the men to come in. Tell Johnny Anthon I asked himself and Conal Andy and Paddy Brian to come, in a hurry.' She went to the door and called to the young people. And she beckoned them to hurry. When they came in she told them what was afoot. 'It would look like we are going to have no trouble

61

in getting the meeting anyway,' one of the girls said, but she was nervous. 'Women were the first to back us everywhere else' the spokesman for the young men said. By now there were angry voices outside as well as the heavy tramp of men. 'We would be sorry if we brought trouble on you,' the girl that came first to the door said. Johnny Anthon led the way in. A rush of women swept forward carrying him ahead of them to the hearth. Men stood by the open door. The women surged forward Farthest back, Hughie leaned against the door jamb, his pipe in his mouth. Johnny Anthon looked at his neighbours. 'What's all this hullabaloo? Don't you see they are only childer?' 'They're about the same age, Johnny Anthon, as the first youngsters I ferried before I took to the hills, And the men I chased about with there were no older. Some of what were in jail were even younger.' Hughie spoke quietly from the doorway. Johnny Anthon was puzzled. He stroked his beard. Mary Jim got her chance and she took over. 'You knew who these others were and they never came in here to tell us do this or do that. There's only one word to say to these playboys and that is to get out. If they don't do that there's only one other choice and that is to load themselves and their tents onto a boat and land them on the mainland. They should be glad to be let off that easy.' But Susan was not going to withdraw her shelter from the youngsters on her floor. She spoke up and said the girls were welcome to sleep in her house and the boys had a right to their say. They should be let tell what brought them. But Mary Jim would not give way. 'Don't set yourself up against the rest of us, Susan Duffy, and if these people want to talk, let them come straight out and tell us is it true or is it not that they are here to make a row about *No Trespass*. Do they or do they not want to tear it down?' One of the boys spoke up. It was true they wanted to throw *No Trespass* in the tide, but they would rather see the people of the island themselves do it. However if they said the word it would be done for them. He and those with him were part of a crusade to save the beaches for the nation. 'If you raise a finger against *No Trespass* it's yourselves that will go into the tide, if it is only the women that have to do it,' Mary Jim stormed. 'You won't do it in our name and we won't let you do it in your own. Go back to your school or wherever you came from.'

Hughie rid his throat and the whole kitchenful of people swivelled round to face him. He spoke across to the students. 'So you came to save us from *No Trespass?*' There was a touch of sadness in his voice. 'We would rather you rose up against it yourselves,' the spokesman said. Nobody more than glanced back at him and for once Johnny Anthon was silent. Hughie Duffy was now speaking for the island. His gaze went back to the students. 'Maybe, like you said, you are part of a crusade. I saw that day too, and you could say it was a *No Trespass* crusade in a way for we wanted to push past the people that stood between us and our country. Our crusade didn't get very far. Cute men that stayed hid were back before we noticed and we were out in the cold, rules round us like barbed wire. Oh, we got scraps through the rules, but an island can't live on scraps. Now you show up, with as little in your heads as we had. If you want to help us go back to Dublin and see if there is anybody looking our way. Cast up at city workers that they turned their backs on us, and warn them that one day they will have need of our kind.'

'Make it easy for us,' a student pleaded. 'Give a signal not alone they but the whole country will see. Tear down *No Trespass.*' His voice trembled. But again people no more than glanced back over their shoulders. They were hanging on Hughie's words now. He put his pipe in his mouth and drew on it to keep it alive. He took the bowl in his palm. 'You're no better and no worse than we were, caught in the make-believe that fooled us. If we're shut in, its rules they made in Dublin has us shut in. I was in one jail and now I'm in another.' He put his pipe back in his mouth and smoked. Mary Jim had her chance to take over. 'Listen to me will you all.' She swept to the front and nudged Johnny aside. Her face was dark with anger. 'Are you all daft? When was it ever so on this island that any-body but youngsters with people in Boston to send them their passage money could get out of it? Now when there's a chance for whole families are we going to let these playboys and whipsters rob us of it? Every family can talk for itself but I went out and I told the T.D. that I wanted my man to sell his house and his land and every four footed animal on it and take himself and us to Boston.' 'But his mother' somebody gasped. 'She would rather live with Kitty anyway, and she has her pension, and we will send her money from Boston.' 'Big Jim would never leave his mother on top of the wind like that,' Kitty scolded. 'It's that or do without a wife. If he wants to have a wife in me he will take me to Boston. By the luck of God the

64

T.D. is an agent for the Anchor Line and he will give us the tickets and wait for his money.' Susan coughed. It was a nervous act for she had no mind to speak but Mary Jim turned on her. 'And I'm warning you, Susan Duffy, to mind your tongue. All I hear from Jim's mother, day in, day out, is look at Susan Duffy. Stay here if you like but don't shelter anybody that would get in the way of the money that would save people like me. Leave the road out clear for us.'

A spokesman for the students sought Hughie's aid. 'What this woman is saying is that the island should empty itself out. That Ireland should empty itself.' 'Ach, Ireland' Mary Jim mocked, 'What have we to do with Ireland? What notice did Ireland ever take of us? Tell them, Hughie Duffy, what Dublin said to you: What the very men you were in jail with said back to you through the T.D.' 'But your T.D. is in the plot to get rid of you' one of the girls fought. She caught Susan's arm. 'Wouldn't it be better for you all if we could go back to Dublin and tell them that you are making a stand for yourselves.'

'Have you wool in your ears girl,' Mary Jim all but screamed. 'Amn't I telling you to scat. All I want and people like me want is a free foot. There is women on this island whispering what I am shouting.'

'Have the men nothing to say' one of the boys asked. Mary Jim rounded on him. 'What do men know about living? Slave away and hand over the few shillings you make. Put your cap on your head and walk out. That's a man for you. Does he see a woman withering or the girl he married turning into a hag?'

'Easy now, Mary Jim' Susan soothed. 'It's not men's fault that the fishing failed. Let the herring come and this island will soon get its heart back and so will everybody on it.' She raised her head and her voice. 'Don't you all mind when the herring used to be here, the shouting and the laughing and the barking of the dogs?' 'There you go Susan Duffy' Mary Jim scoffed, 'what is that but the talk of old people? No wonder your name is for ever on their lips. 'Why can't ye all be like Susan and Hughie; like Susan and Hughie . . . . . .' Her voice crumbled. She covered her face with her stained apron and sobbed and sobbed. Susan moved quickly and put an arm around her. No word was spoken in the kitchen. Mary Jim jerked herself free and wiped her face and with her head high, forced her way to the door. The dumbfounded kitchen fidgetted for a moment and then emptied itself out on her heels.

11

What went on by the fireside when Hughie, Susan and the students were alone together not even Kitty Paddy Brian could find out. One thing was clear next morning. Men did not wish to hold a session on The Green for crews came early, each one hoping to be gone before the next. It was an ease to them all that the three boys were already swimming in Poolban and well out on the edge of the dangerous tide and eddies by the outer crook. Fine how do you do if one of them should get a cramp. That would set up talk. Conal Andy whistled them back and there were few men on The Green but had something to say about them. One of the boys hoisted himself over the stern of a punt, hauled in the anchor, dipped a knowing oar in the water and sent the punt skimming by sculling. A boy that could scull! Here was something to laugh at. That was the boy they made a stranger of last night. As if to rub things in one of the other two, with a towel round his shoulders, stooped on Conal Andy's half darned net and added a few meshes. If the sculling caused a laugh this set up a cheer. 'Blast you' Conal Andy growled, 'why did you hide it from us that you were our own sort?' The Green now was friendly and the men were glad to notice Kitty Paddy Brian nearby for she would take word of this through the island. Johnny Anthon wanted to know if they would like to go out the bay. They would. Johnny Anthon named the crews that would take one a piece. The girls came out on The Green and they, too, were in swimming togs.

There was no further talk of *No Trespass.* They were all fisher folk together, and the young people of the island sent out a hurried call for a dance in a kitchen. The massed band of the island, three melodeons and two fiddles was there. One of the dancers was about to shout 'No Trespass' but he caught himself on in time and whooped 'Mind the dresser.' With a cheer it was taken up and even the students joined in. After a full three days on the island and endless teas the students left. It was noticed that Mary Jim kept out of their way and in no house did they drop a hint that they were upset at the way the island made little of their message. Hughie and Peter Dan rowed them across to the mainland and helped them up the rocks with their packs.

But even while the students made a topic for men, women were whispering. There were some things that could not be talked of aloud. It was quick of Mary Jim to see in this business of Minnie MacBride right from the start that a whole family could now up anchor and away to Boston. And she had aired the truth, too, in what she cast up at the men. They were too willing to wait and make do with what fishing came their way. Another year without herring and there was no telling what grip Mary Jim's idea would take but there was something that caused them to lower their voices and choose when to talk. And that was her sudden burst of crying. What was back of it? There was a laugh in this, for there were women of her age that could think back how Mary Cormac had her eye on Hughie Duffy. There was more than a touch of tantrum in the way she ran off with Big Jim within a few weeks of Hughie marrying Susan. If Mary Jim suffered from any sickness, even as little a thing as a toothache, she would get ready pity, but an upset over love was something to mock. Many a woman made do with a second or indeed a third choice, and no grumble.

Kitty Paddy Brian somehow caught all the whispers. She could read as much into a sudden silence or a stammer as another into a sermon. But she wanted a word from Susan to make everything clear. She hinted that it was being talked of, the way Mary Jim kept out of Susan's way even at the floating shop. Susan was quick, maybe a shade too quick, to raise her voice to tell Kitty there was one tale she could spread and welcome; that there was no falling out between Susan Duffy and Mary Jim. 'Don't you give in that her talking about hightailing for Boston is enough to get her sent to the Big House?' Kitty challenged. Susan really hit back then. 'Whoever said the like, Kitty, best look out. Mocking is catching.' But Kitty Paddy Brian was not easy to silence. 'Ach, Mary Jim maddens me. She is the last woman on the island that should raise her voice. Wasn't she always at the foot of the class at school? What sense is there in the like of her laying down the law?' 'Mary Jim was no dunce. She was no good at sums but she read every book she could get her hands on. Maybe there's where she gets these ideas. For all we know she is maybe a step ahead of us all.' 'Then what about yourself and Hughie? Or is there any truth in what's often said that if everybody's people in Boston kept home in mind like them belonging to you and Hughie it would be easy for everybody to wait for the herring.'

'If you are trying to draw talk out of me Kitty you are wasting your time. I'm not saying but we get money from Boston, but I never touch a penny of it for Hughie has something else in his mind and what's his wish is my wish and I thank God for that.' 'Maybe that's what anchors the two of you to the island so much.' Kitty sighed, 'the wish you have for one another. Whatever it is, the two of you is what holds this island together.' Kitty got wearily to her feet. 'Suppose I do a bit of poking for a change, Kitty. You were in Boston and when Paddy came back you were on his heels and you married him. So why don't you tell us that Boston is not all sunshine.' 'I was in Boston surely and when Paddy Brian had to come home after his father died, I followed him and I married him, and many a night I cried myself to sleep.' 'Then you should be the last to blame Mary Jim so. You ought to be ashamed of yourself.' 'All that was wrong with me was pitying myself and when I got over that I got my heart back. And another thing: a man is not blind just because he keeps his mouth shut. I pity Big Jim.' 'Big Jim is a good man, I always liked him and I told Mary Jim that.' Kitty went to the door and pushed it shut. 'Do you know she all but clawed the eyes out of him the last two times she found herself with child?' 'Whist Kitty for God's sake. That's a thing should be on nobody's tongue and it's a thing Big Jim shouldn't even breathe to you.' 'I didn't hear it from Big Jim. It was his mother got her ear to Mary Jim in a tantrum. And let me say this, and you know it's the truth, except to yourself I wouldn't breathe a word of it, and I'll never break breath with it again.'

'Life can get very ravelled for some people.' Susan spoke slowly. 'God forgive me if I was a bit heedless about Mary Jim. It could be she is to be pitied. It would go to the heart in me, bad feeling to be between her and Big Jim. There was something she all but said to me once.' She faced Kitty. 'I'll take my knitting and I'll go over to Mary Jim this night. Hughie will mind the children and will you see to it that Big Jim's mother is out of the way.' 'She'll be out of the way,' Kitty promised, 'and you'll have the fireside to yourselves, the two of you, for as soon as you sit down there you can be sure Big Jim will put on his cap and head for Hughie. It's the man's way on this island when a neighbour woman comes to his fireside, to light his pipe and make for her's.'

'It's a man's way surely,' Susan agreed. 'God help half the world the way it hides itself from the other. A body could live on this island for a hundred years and never know all about it. I thought I knew Mary Jim through and through.' She picked up the tongs to build a fire. Kitty went out.

But Susan Duffy had no talk with Mary Jim that night. Mary Jim always did her best to keep Kitty within ear shot and she picked up enough to see to it that her sister was perched in the corner, her knitting in her fingers, when Susan Duffy sauntered in. It was a tame night of light gossip.

12

There was nothing in the sky at bedtime to give any warning of the storm that struck before dawn. There was scarcely a grownup that was not startled awake by the roar of it. Roofs trembled and shed dust. Hughie Duffy was quickly out of bed. He opened the sheltered door. A gust of wind eddying round the gable swept in and raised a cloud of ashes from the raked fire. He went outside in his bare feet, holding the door closed behind him. The storm sweeping in from the west, seemed to skid over his roof, sucking at it as it passed and, bouncing on The Green, land with a thud in the sea. But did it clear the boats before it struck? Hughie went back inside. Susan handed him the lighted lanthorn. Seeing the light men knocked and Hughie joined them. He was not the only one afoot.

The two outer boats danced dangerously. They were just beyond the shelter of the high ground, where the blast struck The Green, and vaulted over Poolban, its trailing skirts tugging these two boats. They would have to be brought close into the shelter. There was strength enough in the blasts to sweep a man's legs from under him so men linked arms. For light there was the ragged racing sky and the faint shine of the sea.

If the two outer boats should drag their anchors or snap their cables they would be in the staves on the mainland by morning. Neither of the men who owned these boats was among the first to reach Poolban but what matter. A boat was as much a bit of the island as a man. A boat was everybody's concern. So one of the sheltered boats was manned and after a struggle the two outer ones were brought to safety. The tide was low and that helped. Waves were flinging themselves at the ledge on the North side, but they only came over as spray with no body to them. Seas eddying round at the Southern side were shredded by the scatter of staggered inlets, rocks held together by bleached grasses. 'It's as well there is no boat at Minnie MacBride's this night,' a man said, intending it as a joke. But the men sheltering under the cliff fidgeted: You could tell from the movement of the lanthorns. The Strangers had a boat and *No Trespass* or no *No Trespass* a boat was a boat with rights of her own. Let The Strangers keep to themselves if they wished but a boat must not suffer because of them. Hughie was one of the half dozen who barged their way through the storm to Minnie's inlet. They were only just in time. They managed to get hold of the anchor rope and then getting their hands on the boat drew her up to safety on the grass. A dog barked. A light went on within the house. The island men again with linked arms thrust themselves through the blasts.

In the morning the island woke to find itself in the grip of a hurricane. Cattle had to be foddered in byres and water carried to them in buckets. Children were kept home from school and even grownups kept to the sheltered gables. That night families sat by their firesides. Now and then a stray puff of wind sneezed down the chimney and raised a cloud of ashes. Young people would have made their way over the paths but this first night of storm happened to be All Souls night, one of the two nights of the year when families kept to their own firesides. Old people talked of those long dead. It was the rule to go to bed early and it was the one night of the year when fires were not raked. Instead, a new fire was built at the end of a rosary that had more trimmings to it than ever. It was a lore of the island that the dead could visit their old homes on All Souls night. Maybe nobody believed it, but what harm? The fire was a sign that they were welcome and so let it be.

By morning the wind hadn't eased but the island was no longer housebound. Men and women fought their way to the West shore to see the sea in its rage. Youngsters were afoot earliest for there was always a chance of finding a piece of wreckage even after one night of storm, but what drew the grownups was the white crests of waves mountain high, tearing themselves to spume on sunken rocks and flinging themselves in a sizzle of foam at the buck-toothed shore. There was a wide stretch of open sea to give plenty of space for waves to build themselves up. This was one of the sights of the island, the West bay on the rampage: Breakers mast high in the lunatic patches of sea that had a fury of their own. These were the spots to be wary of even in good weather for, by some trick, the sunken rocks there could goad even a gentle heave of sea to hump itself and spew forth in an onward rush that would swamp a boat and turn her over and over.

There was no hope for a crew caught in such a burst. Old men pointed out these spots easily now for they were the high points of maɔness and they warned children to mark them well and bear in mind for ever the need to beware of them for there was no method to their moods. It meant nothing that they could be like a lake for a stretch for there was no telling what minute madness would work in them. As the devil would have it they were the best fishing grounds around the island and therein lay their main danger.

By nightfall the storm was if anything worse but the island paths came to life. People were foot free. Young men used the staggering blasts for greater horseplay and girls' voices rose in more full-throated *No Trespass.* The elders of the island made their way to Paddy Brian's and on such a night Paddy was at his best. It was only on such a night that he bade each man welcome. He all but thanked them for coming. He piled more and more of his good black turf on the blazing fire. He lit his pipe and passed it round. Man or mortal never saw the like. 'I did, Paddy, and worse.' 'And what about the night we all heard of that stripped the roofs off half the houses of the island . . . .' The elders settled down to check over and add to the lore of the island on hurricanes.

After four days the storm gagged on itself during the night. Old people who went to sleep with its boom in their ears woke at the sudden quiet. Never in living memory had a storm run itself out of breath in such a way. Men tugging at their gallowses unbolted the sheltered doors. Women wriggled into heavy petticoats and thrust their bare feet into men's boots to follow them out. The sky looked as innocent as a June night. The heel of an old moon cast a weak glow across it. There wasn't even a shadow much less a cloud among the stars. Now was the time to shake young people awake and send hurrying to the west side to search for bits of wreckage. On many hearths live embers were pulled together and fanned ablaze to make quick warm drinks for men in a flurry to get out. Within minutes the whole island was full of voices, young men challenging one another to race for the 'first touch.'

For the island had a way of its own for staking claim to cast in. There was no need for a man who found a plank or a cask among the rocks to stand guard over it. All he had to do was to gather a few handfuls of sand and lay them on it to have his claim put beyond question. If he was foolish enough not to move his find above the reach of a rising tide, and an incoming wave washed away the sand, the first claim no longer held and a second claim could be made by whoever chanced by. And it was all in high good humour, for people thought it a great laugh that this man or that did not know enough to make sure that his find was above high water mark. A mainland man could do no worse and that was about as low as an islander could fall. The law which the island made for itself held and no man could cut across it.

But there was more in mind than the bits of wreckage that might drift in. It happened before that storm drove herring shoals within reach. The worry was would the waves flatten themselves enough for boats to go out? There was no sign of any stir among the sea fowl. There was not a gannet in sight. Men searched but they saw no sign of fish.

Sea fowl would not be lazy if the herring were in. But for all that men were sharp eyed and hopeful that the waves would settle down. As it was they had narrowed their white tops to a mane of foam. If they once drew a skin across that, boats could venture out. The shoals might be keeping too deep for the fowl to go into a tizzy over them. By the look of long stretches of the bay it would be safe for boats to go out by nightfall. If the storm could cut itself off in such a sudden way could not the rage go out of the sea as quickly? Anyway with the West bay it was a case of down wind down sea; not like the North bay.

Susan Duffy took no notice of Hughie climbing into the loft at the end of the kitchen and rummaging around there, for he was a man with busy hands and he stored no ends of truck on the loft. It was only when he flung down a herring net that she was startled to cry out with joy, 'herring, there's sign?' He scratched his head. 'I saw nothing, but Peter Dan thinks he saw something.' 'If Peter Dan thinks he saw something there was something to see, that man has eyes like a gannet. Herring! Its the only thing that would bring this island back to its senses.' Hughie searched for his pipe. He plucked a stiff straw from the besom and poked it into the shank. 'Calm yourself woman. It would only take a new puff in the wind no stronger than a puff from my pipe to have the waves breaking through their skin again. Like you, I have great faith in Peter Dan, but I'm not at all sure about the weather. The trouble is would the island leave it to us to prove the bay for herring? I'm afraid if I show myself outside with a net in my arms there will be no holding back the young men of the

island; and some not so young. Big Jim is talking
already and he has Paddy Brian's two sons as bad
as himself.'

'Don't let any talk make you take risks. Mary
Jim's flare up could be nagging at Big Jim and he
might be a bad man to go by, but then again
herring would be the one thing to settle Mary's
mind.'

A woman coughed at the door. It was not
Kitty's cough. Susan knew it however. This was
Fanny Dan, a woman little given to crossing a
neighbour's doorstep. Susan had but time to
whisper the name to Hughie when she walked in.
She was early middle aged, grey haired, fresh faced.
Susan bade her welcome and did her best to make
it look like it was no wonder to see her. She knew
Fanny's story of course. She was a widow, She lost
her man in one of the island storms. She had one
son, Charlie, a fine strapping young man rising twen-
ty who had the good fortune to get a place on
Hughie's crew. He would be the fifth to what had
hitherto been a four man crew.

Susan saw her flow of talk was being wasted.
Fanny was worried and added no word to what
she said. Fanny's eyes were on Hughie. She was
clearly upset. Susan sought to help her. 'Is there
something bothering you, Fanny?' she asked an-
xiously. Fanny spoke harshly aiming her talk at
Hughie. 'I saw Peter Dan take out your boat from
Inner Poolban and put her on the ride in deep
water. I watched him perched on a flag, his two
eyes stuck on the bay; and now this.' She pointed
to Hughie's net on the floor. 'You have it in mind
to search for herring this night?'

'If the sea goes on settling like it is we likely will

78

give it a try.' He spoke lightly.

'I don't want Charlie on the sea this night.'

'Take care what you say Fanny. If you tie too short a tether to Charlie you may waken up some morning to find his bed empty.'

'Isn't that why I watched my chance to come unknownst. He must not know I came to you.'

'God bless us Fanny, you frighten me.' But Hughie raised his hand quickly and Susan was silent. 'I know what's on your mind, Fanny. You're thinking back to that other night. You never let yourself forget it.'

'I'm more than thinking back, Hughie, I'm looking around me and I see what I see, and I hear the venom in every ripple that crackles the rocks. This is a day like that other day, a pet within a storm.' Susan could keep quiet no longer. She laid a hand on Hughie's shoulder. 'Maybe in God's name the island should give itself another day. And it won't if you once go outside with a net on your arm.' Hughie shook his head and she was silent. It was the rule of the island that a man should be the only voice on anything touching on the sea. But Susan was worried. Hughie turned to Fanny. 'You're doing a wrong thing, but I'm going to let you have your way. I can make an excuse. There's a new net there that needs barking and it will make sense to Charlie that I want it made ready in the hope there will be fishing. I'll tell him we're taking his net and we will fish it and he will get his share. But I'm warning you Fanny never come to me on an errand like this again. This time you will have your way.'

'God bless you.' She delayed on the doorstep with a peep to the right and the left. 'You're not to heed her Susan' Hughie said when Fanny had got out of

79

sight. 'She is always risen when this day of the
year comes round. We will have to be careful with
Charlie. Make a fuss of giving him a hand getting
ready the big pot for barking the net in it. I suppose
I'd best go to him.' He was about to shoulder the
net. 'Don't take that outside yet. If you raise a
hubbub you won't be able to check it.' At that
moment Charlie darkened the door. Susan and
Hughie were taken aback. It was just as well Charlie
spoke at once. 'My mother is upset,' he blurted.
'She says nothing but I can see it in her face. I
know its because of the night that is in it.' Hughie
and Susan didn't even glance at one another. 'I was
going to ask you to tell her you were making me
stay ashore to bark the new net,' he stammered.
'To be sure I would rather go out but she wouldn't
shut an eye' Hughie sat wide legged on a chair and
let on to weigh the wisdom of leaving Charlie
behind to bark the net. In the end he came down
in favour of it. Charlie's face lit up and he pleaded
to be let run off with the news to his mother.
'Under God,' Susan said when he was gone, 'does
anybody ever know what is in another's mind?
There they are the two of them playing tig with
one another like children among the stooks in the
stubble field in the moonlight. Still is it not a grand
thing to see so much feeling for his mother in a
boy like Charlie?' She sighed. 'All the same this is
no ease to me, Hughie. Fanny did say she saw the
face of that other day in this day.' 'Ach' Hughie
scoffed. 'She'll see the same face this day twelve
months from now and every twelve month while
she lives.' Susan sighed and turned away. 'Listen,
Susan,' Hughie soothed, 'I will have a word with
Peter Dan and if there is as much as a swither I'll

stay ashore.' Susan followed him to the door. She stepped outside to look around at the sky. It seemed good natured enough. The wind had fallen to a mere sailing breeze. She was still in the doorway when Hughie came back. 'It's Peter Dan's belief that we should have a go but that we will only shoot and haul and be back again long before dawn. Don't let me find you waiting up for me. I always like to come back to a good warm bed.' He picked up the net.

The island saw him and the uproar began. Men shouted at one another and whistled and crews raced to Poolban. Hughie tried to calm them. If they would be said by him no swarm of boats would go out; just a few to make a test. The seas were still a shade too heavy for his liking. But he was only wasting his breath even though he could point to Susan and Charlie making the big pot ready for the barking of the new net and ask them why did they think he would leave Charlie ashore if he had much faith in the night. A chorus of voices broke out around him. The more boats that went out the better the bay would be searched. It was a wide space. Hughie gave up. He would say no word any more against their going out but they must bear in mind that the first of the night could be the best of it. No boat was to do more than make one try.

The men on The Green hanked their nets for easy boarding. Peter Dan and his two uncles kept their nets in his barn. They came up now each with a net on his back and one slung between them. Peter Dan was about Hughie's age, the early thirties. One of his uncles was little older, the other middle aged with the most of his family already in Boston. Big Jim was one of Paddy Brian's crew. He and

Paddy Brian's sons were among the noisiest on The Green. Conal Andy and his boys were there too. Conal Andy was not in the best of humour. He would rather see the bay more settled but since the boys wouldn't hear of staying ashore there was nothing for it but to go with them, but he added his voice to Hughie's that it must be a quick out and back. A cluster of women came onto The Green. They bantered their men that they were not to show themselves in the morning without being in herring scales up to their backsides. Men growled and bade them go home and leave men to their own work. It was all part of the island lightheartedness at a hint of herring. Hughie called out to Susan to get something ready for him and it was taken to mean that the other women should also withdraw. Once the nets were boarded the men would be on their heels anyway for a quick meal. 'It's a mortal sin Hughie not to coax Peter Dan to have a meal with us, a man living alone is likely to do with a hunk of bread and a slug of milk,' Susan worried. 'No wonder he is like a fishing rod. It's the one oddity in him. I can't understand that he will never take a bite in a neighbour's house. You would think he wouldn't make strange with us anyway.' 'Good on you' Hughie laughed, 'You'll soon be the equal of Johnny Anthon for studying. Leave the man alone can't you to be what he wants to be.' They were both eating when a confused tramp of men's feet and a murmur of troubled voices came to the door. Johnny Anthon and Conal Andy pushed their way in, Paddy Brian's arms draped across their shoulders. Paddy Brian elbowed himself free. 'I'm alright, I tell you.' He sat on the chair that Susan placed for him. 'I don't know what came over me. My head just went spinning, spinning, and the first thing I knew I was on the ground.' He pushed back the chair and stood up. 'But I'm alright. Likely its something I ate. God send Kitty doesn't hear of this for if she does . . . . . .'

'Kitty heard, and it's bed for you this night my boy.' Paddy groaned. 'Kitty has the right of it Paddy. There will be plenty of time' Johnny Anthon pleaded. 'I'm on the one word with Johnny Anthon for once Paddy,' Conal Andy chimed in. 'If we had sense we would all do his bidding.' But Conal Andy was shouted down. Susan wanted to hand round tea and bread but the men made excuses. They must hurry home for this and that. Paddy's crew would not listen to Kitty's plea that they should stay ashore. Indeed they were not let speak for Big Jim made himself their voice. He would see to it that they went by Hughie Duffy's words and Johnny Anthon advised Kitty to let them have their way. 'You might as well try to hold back the tide Kitty as the men of this island once anybody says herring.' Conal Andy dug out a naggin bottle of whiskey from an inside pocket and made Paddy Brian take a slug of it. He carried it to ease his breathing. And Johnny Anthon should take a slug for his legs had a way of going numb if the night turned cold. Paddy Brian stumbled crossing the doorstep. Kitty waited for a word with Susan and Hughie. "It's the first time ever that any weakness struck that man. I don't think he ever even had a cold.' 'He'll be himself again in the morning' Hughie told her 'for he's as tough as a gad. All he needs is a good night's rest, and you should thank God that this upset didn't catch him in the bay.' 'God send the island good luck,' Kitty prayed.

Hughie was a bit troubled that Big Jim had taken over Paddy Brian's boat for Paddy's sons were headstrong and Big Jim himself was a shade daring. 'Now who is doing the studying' Susan teased. She moved her three legged stool near Hughie. 'You'll bear in mind your own teaching and do yourself like you told the others. Promise me you will only shoot and haul. Whatever about the others we're not hard pressed.' He put away his half-smoked pipe. He paused by the doorstep on his way out to dip his fingers in the holy water font. He blessed himself and flicked a drop back at her and then drew the door shut.

13

When Susan got the children to bed and had the fireside to herself, she washed her hair. She was sitting with her back to a crumbling fire drying it when the door shot open. The latch had a habit of failing to drop into place so she paid no heed but when a bucket rattled on the gravel outside she got to her feet; it would take more than a breath of air to do that. She hurried to the door. The night had changed. There was no trace now of the good-natured sky of the dusk. Clouds tumbled and whirled across racing stars. Already a faraway bar was moaning. 'Jesus, Mary and Joseph' Susan prayed. She hurried indoors for a bottle of Doon-well water; one of the half beliefs on the island was the Doonwell water shaken against a storm took the venom out of it. Nobody really thought so, but a scared woman doesn't have to believe in the words that old people used to fall back on them in a moment of panic. 'Hughie.' she shouted, 'head for home.' It was just that the words leaped out.

And as though to mock her at that moment a whirlwind blast struck. She hurried to the children to make sure they had not been startled. They were asleep. She gently lowered the blanket from Eoin's head. Her thoughts were as restless as her fingers and her feet. The men were sure to have seen the night threaten storm. It was because she was by the fire without heed or notice of what went on outside that she saw no sign of change. The boats would be racing back under wings of sail by now with the wind behind them. She piled turf on the fire. Hughie had asked her to have the bed warm but he would know she could not shut her ears to what was going on. A good fire would be his first need. Her hands fumbled as she picked up the tongs to build a new fire. It was loose-jointed. That was one thing that needed mending, that same tongs, with its weakness for one leg crossing the other. She knew she was making a fuss over the tongs to keep herself from fright. She told afterwards how Donal came to the room door and she had to chase him back to bed and stretch herself beside him until he slept. She tiptoed back to the kitchen, snatched a shawl from a peg on the end gable and went out. She saw to it that the latch went home.

The fire on the hearth was in ashes when the door was pushed open and Kitty and Paddy Brian came in. 'This bed was never slept in' Kitty said. 'This fire was never raked' Paddy added. Kitty tiptoed to the bedroom. The children were fast asleep. She came back to the kitchen where Paddy was picking live embers of coal to start a new fire. Kitty took the tongs from his hand and he went for an armful of turf from the creel at the weather door. 'She'll be a block of ice' he whispered. Kitty kept her voice low too. 'I saw her below at Poolban I took my eye off her and when I looked again she was gone. Boats came in, one after the other out of the darkness, but not Hughie's. I would be afraid the last of the boats is in. She would be saying to herself: the best boat and the best crew. Hughie's boat could not be the one not to come back. Fine I can tell that's what she'd be saying to herself.' Kitty still kept her voice low, the sleeping children only part of the cause. She filled the kettle and hung it on the crook over the fire. Paddy knelt on the hearth and puffed at the coals. The dry turf caught flame. He rose, dusting his knees. Just then the door crashed open and a clump of sou'westered men staggered in on the floor, Susan in their midst. Kitty rushed to her and half carried her to a seat in the corner. Susan buried her face in her hands. Her tears fell, but there was no sound. 'You're foundered,' Kitty fussed. She fixed up the fire under the kettle. She laid down the tongs and faced the men. They were bareheaded and silent. And then Susan spoke. 'I stood there among the neighbours.' Her voice was scarce above a whisper. 'Boats came in one by one but no Hughie. I withdrew myself into the dark to cry for my heart told me he was not coming. It was the right of other women to be happy when their men came in and not have to hold themselves in check because of me.' Kitty raised her head to gainsay Susan but the faces of the men checked her. 'How could it happen?' she asked helplessly. 'I was the last he spoke to' Johnny Anthon said. 'He came close to me and told me to haul and head for home and right enough I was already suspicious of the night myself for the sea beneath me was uneasy. He asked if anybody was out closer to the danger spots and I told him only Big Jim and Paddy Brian's boys.'

'I'll chase them home,' he said, ' haul and be off. '
That was the last I saw of him, and the last word
anybody heard from him. I made the boys do as he
bid and I had to get a shade cross with them before
they would give in. We were on the last net when
Big Jim hailed us going by. I had a word with him
and I told him that Hughie was away out looking
for them and Big Jim whistled. Hughie would know
that whistle. It was then like you would clap your
hands that a wave rose up and burst open in white
foam.and came galloping down on us. The last net
was no more than cleared in over the side by this
time. We backed water for our lives, stern on to the
boiling wave. Conal Andy and Big Jim were no
more than a length or two ahead. The breaker
was in its last gasp when it got to us but for all that
it gushed in and all but swamped us. There would
be no hope, no hope in the world for a boat further
out. The brig Eliza could not live through yon. We
sat on our oars. We waited and we shouted. There
was no sound but the new roar of breakers, for by
now the whole sea was up. Much as I hate to say
it . . . .' his voice broke. 'The last crew a body
would name of all the boats that go out from this
island to be the one that got caught . . . . But then
wasn't he the one most likely to do what was
done, to go out like yon after neighbours in danger.
And they did not even have to be neighbours.'
Johnny Anthon wiped his face with the inside of
his sou'wester.

Kitty handed Susan a bowl of tea. She pushed it
aside. 'It would choke me,' she said. Donal peeped
out of the room door. He was taken aback to see
all the men. He searched among the faces for his
father. Susan got to her feet and knelt to put her

arms around him. She staggered as she got up from her knees and turned to face the silent throng. 'There's nothing anybody can do now," she said quietly. Her second child came to the doorway. She lifted him in her arms and holding Donal by the hand, frowned at the neighbours to hold them silent. Kitty's eyes went from face to face among the men, and every face told the same story. 'Then in God's name leave her to her children.' They went out slowly. Mary Jim was the last to go.

he island never knew how
Susan broke the news to the
children that their father was
lost but Kitty who was first in
on the floor next morning told
how the four were gathered
round Susan in the corner
when she opened the door.
She was at a loss to know what to say when Donal
spoke up and told her — and it was almost a boast
— that their father went to save other men and was
drowned. 'Ma says that she will make shadows on
the wall now and tell us stories.' Eoin chimed in.
Kitty could see that Susan had trouble to keep a
grip on herself. She spoke quietly to the children.
'You'll be good now, won't you, and do as Kitty
bids you until I get back.' Kitty put a firm hand on
her shoulder. 'The word is that you are to stay
where you are. The whole island is strung around
the shore. As soon as there is any news somebody
will run to you with it.' Susan stiffened for a moment and it looked like she would brush off Kitty's
hand, but Nellie was clinging to her skirt, asking her
not to go, and she took the child in her arms and
sat down. 'It's not as if I had any hope' she
whispered.

A cluster of women came to the door and Kitty

hurried to meet them. She gestured them back. Outside the doorstep she told them that Susan did not want any upset to the children. Some of the women did not take that in good part. There was a special way of doing it. They pushed past Kitty only to find themselves face to face with a roused Susan. 'Chokin' to the lot of you' she said in a harsh whisper. 'Don't you see these?' She jerked her head to the children. 'You'll have to forgive me,' she added wearily 'but I have trouble enough with myself as it is but I have to keep a hold on myself because of them.' The children, sensing something was wrong came to her and pressed against her. 'I have to be father and mother to them from now on.' One women glanced at the other. It was Mary Jim who spoke up to say that everything should be as Susan wanted it. She led the way out. They halted by the gable. Some felt they had been cheated and they grumbled. This was not the island way to behave at a time like this. It was Mary Jim who now spoke again to say that Susan's word must be law. What kind of law is it? Was there ever a drowning where there was a stop put on women crying their eyes out? At no drowning within memory or beyond had the island been denied its oldest right in such a bare-faced way.

Kitty for once found herself on one word with Mary Jim, but gave in that she, too, was puzzled. And what was more she was afraid that Susan Duffy was keeping too tight a hold on herself. There was a lot of wisdom in the island habit of crying its dead. It would do Susan good to cry. It was the natural thing to do. But Susan was standing guard over her children and right or wrong the island must be said and led by her. Her time for crying would come.

A boy raced up with word that the capsized boat had been sighted and that a mainland motor boat was bearing down on her to tow her ashore. Mary Jim hurried back with the news to Susan. 'You stay with the children, Mary.' Susan set off for the shore not even waiting to snatch a shawl. Kitty kept pace with her and tried to force her own shawl on Susan's shoulders but she thrust it aside. By now there were whistles, voices, shouts. Susan was sobbing as she ran. A woman took her arm but let it go, she said afterwards it was as dead as a piece of rope.

The motor boat was in among the waves where they still tumbled white-crested. Susan stood on a bare flag and neighbour women as they came up closed in around her to give her shelter. Men, wise in how best to take a capsized boat in tow, shouted without any hope of making themselves heard that they agreed among themselves that, from what they saw, the motor boat crew knew what they were about. They got a light grappling iron across the swamped boat to turn her right side up but she rolled over and fell back. A groan went up from the women. There had been no doubt from the start whose boat it was but for all that the sight of the blue gunwale was like seeing a face. The crew of the motor boat got a better hold and the righted boat did not fall back this time. She was towed close enough for a cable to reach the shore, and soon men were able to wade into the water and take hold. There were so many hands there was scarce space for them. The boat, splashing water, was beached. There were no bodies, no oars, no nets. Even the loose thwart was gone as also the floor boards. The women of the island could have their way now and they gave full vent to the traditional way of island lament. Only Susan was silent. When the empty boat was beached she walked down and rested her hands on the bow rowlock. Hughie always sat on that oar. She turned away home. Nobody followed her.

There was a blazing fire. Mary Jim sat among the children who squatted on the hearth each with a bowl of crumbed 'shop' bread and hot milk. The table was piled with gifts. There was a row of jugs of milk. Mary Jim rose and pointed to the children. 'There's your world now, Susan, I have to say it. I begrudged you everyone of them. So now you know. I can talk now for I opened my heart to Big Jim last night, and God help him, he had his own cross to bear. It will be alright between us from now on. But you and Hughie were made for one another. Big Jim and me, we both knew it.' Her voice was little more than a whisper. Donal offered a spoonful from his bowl to his mother and she swallowed it. They embraced and the children looked at them in wonder. She sat by the fire and leaned against the bed. Mary Jim tip-toed out and left her alone with her children.

Kitty made a round of the houses, People should get into their heads that Susan Duffy's only reason for keeping them at arm's length was that she wanted to shelter her children and, maybe, a good bit herself. If she broke down once she would find it hard to pull herself together again. It looked to Kitty that what was keeping her together now was likely a vow she made to herself to do as Hughie would have wished. There was no telling even what to say to the children before her. The right thing to do was to let her shut herself off for a while, and Kitty took her own advice.

Peter Dan's only sister was in Boston; that was all of a family there was. One of his drowned uncles left no family. The other had a son to take over the old home. That house at least was open and people were free to let themselves cry there without let or hindrance.

But while Susan chose to hush everybody that came in on her floor she soon found that the world would not be hushed. The island's name was again in the newspapers. The T.D. brought a man Susan knew by sight. He was a newsman and he had a camera. For the moment he was having a rewarding spell for the drownings were a rich source of news. No doubt other newsmen would come later, meanwhile this was his harvest. He and the T.D. waylaid Susan on her way from the spring well. The world would want to help her but that would depend a lot on how the story was told. He would do his best to make a good fist of it. Susan stood with a full bucket of water dragging at her arm and listened. The T.D. said it would be wise of her to let her picture be taken with the children so that the country might see the burden she had to put up with. His choice of words was not to her liking and she turned on him angrily and said that if that was the kind of world it was, she wanted no help from it. 'Burden indeed.' She let her anger spill over on the T.D. himself and she taunted him with failing Hughie. If the island had the boats Hughie wanted the men would not be in such a fever to risk themselves. But Dublin wouldn't listen to Hughie and what did the T.D. do about it? Hughie said he never opened his mouth in the Dail. This

94

now was Hughie talking and when she found her tongue she lashed at the T.D. with Hughie's words. If all the T.D.s in the country with islands in their care were like him it was a poor lookout. Anyway how would men from the inside of counters, or teachers, or doctors know what an island needed. And as far as the newspapers were concerned this would be only an hour's wonder. She would not make a peep show of herself and the children. If the newspapers had no errand to the island but to write stories about it let them look around and write.

The T.D. had trouble getting the newsman, for all that he was a friend, to see that it would do harm to let any talk seep out that might give the idea that Susan was half crazed. It would put a stop to help for her. He made up a story that would have been worthy of Johnny Anthon, and he got the good natured newsman to agree to use it, and Johnny Anthon to be sure, was on hand to help. It was he got Mary Jim to group her children round her for a picture to go with the story. Anyway there was not much risk of discovery for Mary Jim and Susan were about an age and the island could be trusted on a matter like that to hold its tongue. Besides Mary Jim could dress herself close enough to Susan's way to get by. The word went round that the strange newsmen were to be kept in the dark. This work was made easy by Susan herself for she was in no mood to see strangers although she knew nothing of how the island was standing guard over her.

Johnny Anthon praised the island for how it played its part. The newspapers opened a fund and the pictures were a big help. To be sure the money

95

that came in was for all the families of the drowned men but most of it was earmarked for Susan. The newsmen did themselves credit for they drew on Synge's Riders to the Sea for an idea of what a stricken island was like and the public loved it.

By Sunday the bodies had not yet been found and the congregations at all the masses put their hearts into prayer that the sorrowing families might be given the comfort of seeing their men buried in holy ground. A crowd waited by the chapel gate to catch a sight of Susan as she came out from the church — a tallish, black haired woman, that didn't even pull the shawl over her head to hide her pale face. The islanders did not stand around nor go into shop nor public house but hurried back to their boats. By the early afternoon the sea was dotted with boats and the newsmen got good pictures. Spots of the sea were still lumpy. Nothing came of the search.

It was almost a week before the bodies were found, Peter Dan's first, and then the others within hours. Johnny Anthon, with Conal Andy and Paddy Brian on his heels, brought the news to Susan. They had to tell her that the bodies were already coffined. She closed her eyes but took the news calmly. Her first wish was to have Hughie's coffin brought to his own home but she let herself be talked into agreeing that the crew should be waked as one. The four coffins were laid side by side in the schoolhouse. There was word that a man from the mainland would have to come before the burial could take place. He came, a friendly man, who asked this and that about how they died and then made a speech about the bravery of Hughie Duffy and his crew and the need for a better system of weather guidance for island fishermen. He said the country didn't pay enough heed to these islands. They should be proud of them, places that could rear such heroes. Then the T.D. made a speech and the islanders liked what he said for he too spoke well of them.

Johnny Anthon took it on himself to praise the T.D. for how much he put himself out to help the island in every way and especially in these days of its sorrow. 'If that doesn't put Johnny Anthon in high favour with the T.D. Paddy,' Conal Andy whispered, 'nothing will.'

The funerals were the largest that ever went out from the island for boats from other islands joined in. At the chapel gate the whole countryside were gathered, and more pictures were taken. Strangers jostled one another for a view of Susan on her way in and out of the graveyard.

The T.D. was back on the island next day. He wanted the address of Peter Dan's sister so that he might wire her a message of sympathy. The idea of a telegram to America was new to the island and it was a wonder to them that the T.D. could say he had a reply from Boston by the next day. But by now people learned that he had something more than sympathy in mind. He had a buyer for Peter Dan's place.

Conal Andy roused himself to say that a claw of his land, a scrabby patch worth nothing, cut across the top of the landing place of Peter Dan's. He had all but forgotten about it for indeed he had no call to think of it while Peter Dan lived. What put it into his head now was that these new people might put up another *No Trespass* on it. And right enough Conal Andy's talk brought the

97

T.D. back next day with a map that showed Conal Andy's finger of land. The people buying Peter Dan's place told him to say they would be glad to pay a fair price so as to have a clear way to the shore. It was lucky for Conal Andy that Johnny Anthon was with him just then, for Conal Andy put no value at all on the rush riddled patch and it was on the tip of his tongue to say so when Johnny Anthon tramped on his foot. Conal Andy lit his pipe and left the talking to Johnny Anthon. The T.D. made an offer and Conal Andy was about to agree with him when Johnny Anthon tramped on his foot a second time. The T.D. raised the price by ten pounds and Conal Andy feeling a bit ashamed of himself brushed Johnny Anthon aside. It was a good price and whoever the buyer was could have the strip. Anyway Peter Dan's inlet was no place for a boat, and Poolban was only a cable length away.

The map also showed that a slice of Johnny Anthon's land cut into the upper reaches of Peter Dan's field. There was land belonging to Peter Dan mixed in with Johnny Anthon's and a swap was made which was greatly in Johnny's favour. What the buyer of Peter Dan's place had in mind was to have a clear field that he could fence, a wire fence. That would leave people no choice but to bend their paths where the fence got in their way.

The T.D. looked towards Susan's house every now and then but there was no sign of her and Johnny Anthon advised him he had best keep out of her way for a while longer.

Amidst of all these goings on, Susan's name was seldom off women's lips. What was to become of her? There were stories about the money that was

coming to her from the newspapers. She had the
T.D. to thank for that. She had a right to go out
of her way to show it, instead, from the odd word
she spoke, it was clear that she had no wish to
see the man good or bad. It looked like there was
much more in Hughie's talk against the T.D. than
men knew and that it was working itself out now
through Susan. But let her treat the T.D. as she
liked she had no right to keep the island at arm's
length as she was doing. The day would come
when she would have to come down out of the
clouds, and people would maybe have these days in
their nose for her. The money from Boston and
whatever she got of this other money would not
last forever. Let her take care the time would not
come when she might be glad to have the T.D. on
her side. So far, all people knew for certain was
that she was sending letters to Boston and getting
letters back but nobody knew what was going on.
A fine how-do-you-do in a place where a letter from
Boston was as open as a newspaper.

Johnny Anthon and Conal Andy and Paddy
Brian were in and out on the floor often to light
their pipes. Sometimes they even sat and that was
new. At night a woman or two looked in on her
but talk was not easy because of the children, and
probe as they would they could not pick up a word
that it was worth while to say over again to others.
Indeed a good deal of the time they were with
Susan her carryon was for the children casting
shadows on the wall with her hand, a skill for men.
She showed them how the secret lay in having the
lamplight touch the hands in a certain way; as if
they cared . . . . . .

Now and then one came near to asking her straight

99

out about this and that to force from her some hint of how she looked on the years ahead but she gave away nothing. They lost patience with her, especially when she let on not to know what Peter Dan's sister got for her land; a likely story, when Hughie's people in Boston lived only a few doors from her. Fine they would know and they would not be without letting her know, too, but the word they got back from their own people in Boston was that it was as hard to get a word from there as it seemed to be to get anything out of Susan. Wouldn't it madden anybody not to know how much a woman in Boston got for her land and besides have to thole the let on by Susan that she did not know. No woman on the island ever before kept her mind so much in the dark.

Then one day the T.D. came in to see Susan and he spoke boastfully of his errand. He had a paper with him for her to read so that she could see he had not sat on his hands. Here was a letter and it would open up a new life for her. She was to be given a home on the mainland, free gratis and for nothing, with fenced in fields around it and two cows. The thing for her to do, to be sure, was to sell her own place on the island. Lucky for her it would fetch a great price because of Poolban and with that money on top of what else was coming to her she would be well set up for life. Then, too, on the mainland there would be a better chance for the children; better schooling. But he came back to The Green in a sour. He was not at all pleased with the way Susan took his message. The island would have to talk to her. He couldn't. The island should take her in hand like it was all set to bustle Minnie MacBride with its advice. He put it straight to

Johnny Anthon.

And Susan? 'Honest to God, yon woman is out of her mind' was the story that went out. Nobody asked who began it. 'Do you know what she asked the T.D.? What was done with the people that were on the land I'm to get?' 'Like the man said you would swear it was a trap was being set for her and not a favour to her.' But the T.D. held a check on his annoyance. 'The people in Dublin bought the land from the old pair on it. Their two sons in Glasgow agreed to let it go.' 'That was a thing Hughie often said' says she back saucy as you like, 'the mountainy people are faring no better than us. He was round the mountains and kept himself in touch.' She thanked the T.D. but he wasn't taken in by her. He knew it was only a make-believe kind of thanks. She said she would have to let Hughie's people and her own people in Boston know and get their advice.

The T.D. was back next day. It was now his turn to press Johnny Anthon for help. Dublin was looking for an answer and he did not know what to say. Had Johnny done his best? Was it not plain to the world that fenced land with a house and cows could give her a good way of life? There would be the money he would get for her every week over and above what was coming to her from the papers and the price of her farm. And these people were at him to hurry things up. If he kept them waiting longer they might sheer off. Johnny Anthon promised to help but he was more between two minds than the T.D. knew, and Conal Andy was full of doubts too. He couldn't put his finger on it but there was sense in Susan sniffing at this offer on the mainland. Why were the others leaving it to

101

make room for her. 'Hughie often said . . . . .'
There it was, Hughie's guiding hand and who would
try to brush that hand aside, not Susan.

One thing the T.D. said worried Johnny Anthon
and Conal Andy did not gainsay him on it. Susan
Duffy might well be asking herself what would
happen to the island if it lost Poolban. The T.D.
had the right of it when he said she was to put that
thought out of her head. The island was ragged
with inlets, none of them like Poolban, to be sure,
but useable. The only drawback — and it was a big
drawback — was that boats had to be beached for
safety everywhere except at Poolban. Susan was
one that could very well hurt herself thinking of
others.

To add to Johnny Anthon's trouble, Conal
Andy brewed another suspicion of the T.D. and it
was that he had an iron of his own in the fire.
Maybe he had his mind on the fat penny that
could come to himself from selling Duffy's of
Poolban. He would blow up the getting of this
farm outside until it would be a big help to him in
the next election. He could have that in mind. But
there could be another thing. Would the T.D. be
afraid that with the money coming to her and what
she had in the stocking she would open a shop?
There were no flies on the T.D. when it came to
number one, and if there were his grandmother
would whisk them off. They were a cute lot.

Johnny Anthon thought of it. 'I have to give in
Paddy that Conal Andy has this thing studied like I
never knew him to study anything. I give in too,
that the T.D. would not be above thinking such a
thing. I had the same thought myself and now
Conal Andy has it, so would it not be natural for

102

the T.D. himself to have it? But go over this and that as much as I like, Paddy, I came down on the T.D.'s side in the end. It's against my toes but I do.'
Fenced land and a firm road under your feet was something not to be sneezed at.

But then what would Susan do with land? Land needs to be in strong hands and a woman's strength would be no match for it with the heather for ever nibbling its way back. If it was any other woman a body could say she would pick herself a man, one used to land, but not Susan. They were at one on this, that you could take your bible oath Susan would never marry again. And then she would be lonely on the mainland, for after the children her heart was stuck in the island. It was a hard thing to be sure to say to her do this or that.

And talking of land, were they losing sight of the good fields Susan had on the island? It would be no bad idea if somebody was to say to her — and here is where Paddy Brian's Kitty would come in — that the men on the island would gather to her every Spring and again at the harvest and cut her turf as well as thatch. Then, too, if God sent the herring more than one boat would fish a net for her. Johnny Anthon all but talked himself over to Conal Andy's side.

Mary Jim was all against the fenced farm but she had a way of her own for it. And it came out of a friend for whatever rift was between them was gone. They were together again like of old. People wondered how much of Susan's mind was in Mary Jim's talk. 'If Susan has to leave the island she should go to Boston to be with neighbours and where neighbours could join her, and not to the mainland among strangers.' Not only did Susan and

Mary Jim visit one another but they often sat together at the spring well for a long time. Kitty did her best to get her ear to what they said and she had a mind to steal up close but there were too many watching. One day she did take her bucket and set out openly and the other two women joined her and were full of talk but not as much as one word of what they said was worth carrying away. 'The thing that puzzles me,' Kitty said, 'is that Mary Jim could have such a hold of her tongue. I never knew her to keep a thing behind her teeth before.'

Again the T.D. came back. He was foolish enough to give himself a thin excuse. The paper Conal Andy signed got mixed up with some others and he couldn't lay his hand on it, and the family buying Peter Dan's place were in a hurry. They were friends of those others, and visiting between the two houses would be done by boat only. People listened and were silent but nobody was taken in. Then the real reason came out. He took Johnny Anthon, Conal Andy and Paddy Brian aside to hear what headway they had made with Susan. The man with an eye on her place didn't even need to come to see it. The Land Commission map was enough for him. So far as the T.D. could make out, Poolban need not be lost to the island; only The Green. This drew Conal Andy on him. What use was Poolban without The Green? Let there be no make-believe about that, and let the T.D. get through his head, that the island made it clear to Susan it could live without Poolban. 'Then why don't you tell her to sign and be done with it? If the island has that much of a wish for her it should be at her not to let this offer from Dublin slip through her fingers.' And Johnny Anthon gave in that maybe they should go with the T.D. to Susan and make it clear to her that they were on the T.D.'s side. At least that they were not asking her to hold on to Poolban.

Susan made them welcome. If, as the T.D. said, she would get twice as much as Minnie MacBride, it was a great deal of money and she was thankful to him but, for all that, she could not sign any paper. They were all forgetting one thing. Hughie said *No Trespass* would never go up on The Green. The T.D. lost his patience with her. Here he was slaving away to help her but no more than a mule she wouldn't budge. What was the sense in tethering herself and her children to the island with nothing but hardships facing her and them, and only a careless word of Hughie's as her excuse. To be sure she had the world's pity. It was a great cross to her to lose Hughie, but soldiers were killed, fishermen were drowned, and life has to go on. Susan agreed with him. It was just that she had to wait on word from Boston before she could sign any paper.

15

usan Duffy's name was more and more on the lips of the women of the island and there was less and less pity in the talk that went with it. She was a puzzle to people who liked to see life whole. If she cried her eyes out and went over and over her story again and again she would keep her old place but closing her mind so that there was no telling what went on in it was not the way to carry on with the neighbours. There was no falling off in traffic to the house for woman after woman walked hopefully in on her floor but no one got a worth while word. So grumbles spread and sharpened, but it was no good sheering away. It was agreed that the thing to do was to keep on her heels for she could not go on forever listless as a log drifting in the tide. Something would happen to make her talk.

It was not that Susan had no talk in her. Among the women in the boat going to Mass on Sunday there was nobody with as much to say about sick children or newly dropped calves. That was the maddening thing about her, this readiness to talk about things so far out from her own thoughts. No word that touched on them was let drop. She was among a group going in the church door when the priest put a hand on her shoulder and asked her to step round with him to the sacristy. Kitty Paddy Brian held back until the sacristy door closed behind them. It was clear enough from that, that whatever the priest had in mind it would be no more than a whisper between the two of them.

To be sure Susan knew the priest well, a frail kindly man who usually held the island station at Duffy's of Poolban. He was one of the first from the mainland in to her after Hughie's death and he was in a boat searching for the bodies. 'I'm in a bit of trouble, Susan,' he said in his gentle way. 'The T.D. is not at all pleased about you holding out on taking this place he is getting for you on the mainland. He is at me to say a word to you about it and advise you to take it. I said I would talk to you but that's as far as it went.'

'I suppose in a way I'm not open with him, but Hughie had no high opinion of him. What makes me laugh myself mostly is that Conal Andy thinks he wants me out of the island for fear I will use the money from the papers to open a shop. If he has that in his mind I would like to let him live with it for a while. I suppose the plain truth, Father, is I don't like him and it would go against the grain in me to be said by him in anything after how little fight he made for Hughie; not that Hughie ever blamed him much; Hughie used to say he was a backward poor man.'

'I know you well enough Susan to speak out my mind if I had anything on it. Between the two of us I have no great opinion of this man more than Hughie had, but a body has to be fair to him. This idea of his is not bad. He says the island is holding on to you because of Poolban. I think that was what I was to talk to you about, Poolban.' 'He doesn't know the island, Father, and he doesn't know Johnny Anthon if he thinks it is Poolban. There is not a spot in the world like where our house stands. Hughie was very proud of it. I haven't said it to anybody yet, indeed I'm not clear myself in what I have in mind but . . . .' 'Don't say it Susan ' the priest broke in quickly, 'it's never wise to say a thing until you are sure of yourself. If the time comes that you want a word with me I'm always here.' He smiled at her. They were both silent for a moment. 'Ach, it was a great pity if it was God's Will . . . . .' He stopped himself and took a pinch of snuff. 'You're lucky to have the backing of Hughie's people and your own and you're blessed in the children.' 'I have another blessing too, Father, I have nothing but joy to look back on.' 'You'll make your way, Susan. There is mettle in you. Indeed in the whole island let its people go where they will.' He got to his feet. 'You won't forget I'm here if you need me.' They shook hands. He was still holding her hand when they came out the sacristy door.

The people of the island said short prayers at their own folks' graves that day and then hurried over to Hughie's grave. Susan was still on her knees and they knelt around her. Men and women of the mainland joined them. There were many who had not seen Susan before. A crowd standing farther back looked on. They expected a noisy scene, with wild weeping. Susan did not hide her tears but beyond that she kept her grief to herself. She did not even seem to notice the people around her. It looked as if she was taken aback when she staggered to her feet and saw them. Then she did a strange thing, a thing more in keeping with the world's idea of an island woman. She dropped on her knees and pressed her forehead against the cold earth. This time she had to be helped to her feet. Mary Jim linked her to the chapel gate. The gathering made way for her, murmuring their pity but jostling one another for a sight of her.

It was one of those Sundays when the tide suited for a landing place close to the chapel. There were half a dozen or so boats. Mary Jim guided Susan to a seat in Johnny Anthon's. There was a throng of women in it already for they judged she would travel by it. Would she tell them what passed between her and the priest? That was the whisper among them as she drew near. But all she said was that the T.D. asked the priest to advise her to take the place on the mainland. Conal Andy was there and he was quick to give voice. 'Some day I'll break that man's back.' Again a silence fell. A woman here and there frowned at a man to hold his tongue. They wanted to use the silence to squeeze more talk out of Susan. She didn't even draw her shawl over her head but she said nothing. She was one of the first out of the boat at Poolban. The others were in no hurry. They wanted her out of the way so that they could speak freely. So she was still up to her old tricks, hiding her mind. What had got into her at all? Many a woman in her place would talk and talk and gather the neighbours round her to listen. It was not as if they did not want to help. If she had a mind to open a shop, as Conal Andy hinted, this was a poor way to begin. Maybe it was not for nothing that she whitewashed every year. Maybe she was a bit more uppity than people ever thought, else why didn't she say straight out what was in her head? Once again it was Mary Jim who raised a voice on Susan's behalf. If Susan wanted no help but what her people in Boston gave her and her own good sense who had a right to say a word against her? But Mary Jim didn't get far until somebody cast up at her that she was the one first to barge Susan Duffy, and on her own floor at that; with Hughie Duffy listening to her.

Mary Jim shut her eyes tight and there was a hint of tears in them. 'I drew that on myself but let me say this: I have the fewest halfpence of you all to spend but if Susan Duffy opens a shop she will get every last one of them — while I'm here' she added darkly. Nobody was in a mood to throw angry words around. Susan Duffy was enough to have on their minds. Kitty Paddy Brian had something to say. Susan was always a distant kind of woman except with old people but she was a woman that kept her wits about her. Who but herself would bear in mind in all her sorrow to warn Johnny Anthon not to forget the lamp? But Johnny Anthon and Conal Andy were of the opinion it would be against Susan's nature to make a penny out of her neighbours. They couldn't see her behind a counter. But it would be their wish that she should somehow manage to stay among them where they could keep an eye on her. If there was a fence to be mended or a cow's stake she would only have to say the word And her crops would be the best cared for on the island. Men listening nodded. The women withdrew and spread out over the paths.

16

Somehow the word got around that the next letter that came to Susan from Boston would settle things one way or the other. A letter came and no sooner was the stamp noticed in the Post Office than the word got out. To be sure the least people could do would be to let it reach her before somebody tried to get a word out of her. So they watched and waited. When the time came who should go to her, and would there be any need for an excuse? There would be no good in just walking in to ask her straight out what was in the letter; anyway who would do the like? Kitty Paddy Brian would be the best to pick out of her but for once she held back. 'You might trip over herself with the hurry to that women and have nothing for your race,' she told them. In the end Mary Jim took it on herself to go. She let herself be talked into some make-believe errand. Since it was the day before the shop there would be nothing strange in her going for the loan of a cup of sugar. Mary Jim did as she was bid and she did not keep the island long waiting, nor did she have to whisper her news. 'Hold your tongues till I tell you. Hughie's people and Susan's came together in Boston and they settled it among themselves that the best thing they could do for Susan was to take herself and the children out to them. They were sending her the tickets and they would have a house ready for her to walk into, and what was more there was no stop on Mary Jim spreading the news. In no time at all Susan's kitchen was swamped with a rush of men and women for the like of this had never happened on the island, a whole family lifted out of it at one go.

As soon as they could rid themselves of the hubbub they settled down to let Susan have her say and she vexed them. She still was between two minds on certain things and did not say whether that was a swither as between Boston or the T.D.'s offer. Here, as before, there was the ready word from Mary Jim. It was Susan's choice, she had to live with it. Her own choice would be neighbours in Boston rather than strangers on the mainland. Susan listened but she did not seem to pay much heed.

How the T.D. got the news so quickly nobody knew but he was in bright and early next morning; he got the loan of a motor boat. And he was loud-voiced. Susan should give him leave to send a telegram to her people in Boston to claim their money back. No need to waste it on tickets. He would give them to her and wait on the price of her place to get paid. There would be a good penny over for herself. Surely everybody could see that that was the sensible thing to do. But Susan was not forthcoming. There was still that stiffness in her, that was always there when she faced the T.D. The people in Boston made no mention of selling, The T.D. lost his temper and indeed the people

112

who crowded in on his heels, thought he had cause. He challenged her to say what sense would be in her not selling? The people in Boston were no fools and they wouldn't thank her if she went to them and they got to know later that she let them throw away their money. Who would be daft enough to walk out and leave an empty house behind? And these other people on his books could not be held on a string forever. This chance might pass and there was no telling when there would be another. But it was all a waste of breath. He could get no word out of Susan. Then he tried another line. This money that was paid in to the newspapers by people that were sorry for her had to be kept in mind. They might take a poor view of it if they heard she had run out of the country. They could think it was on their money she emigrated and his name was a lot mixed up with that money. Emigration was a football in politics.

'You have your own trouble surely' Susan said quietly. If there wasn't a sting in the words, people never heard words with a bite in them. But the T.D. was not to be put off that easily. The man that had his eye on this place could be a blessing to the island. He was rich. He had his heart set on Poolban although he only saw it from the sea. He made out that the view from here must be one of the best in the country. And this time Susan had to agree. Many a time herself and Hughie stood in the door watching the mountains change colour and they with an eye on their children playing on The Green. Hughie had a habit of putting his shoulder to the door jamb at dusk on a Summer's evening and many a time he called to her in a hurry to catch sight of a shadow wearing a fringe like a

113

paisley shawl crossing a hill. That was part of the riches that life gave her; the memories of Hughie at the door and the shouts of the children at play on The Green. There was no money in the bank could equal it. Women looked at one another. This was talk such as never passed between them. No wonder the T.D. could make neither head nor tail of her for no woman who had lost her man made so much talk of the joy of their days together and so little of her loss. It was not decent. Come to think of it nobody ever saw her weep, and seldom with as much as a tear in her eye. Was all this a put on to keep the T.D. guessing? Maybe she was not as foolish as she sounded and that this was her way of upping the price. If so let her take care. The T.D. was fast losing patience and by now the island was on his side and not her's.

Johnny Anthon saw the danger and though he was as puzzled as the next and even a shade vexed with Susan he put in a word to shelter her. 'Aren't we all losing sight of what this woman went through, and isn't it clear in what she says that she needs more time.' He faced the T.D. 'This island is maybe not giving her the help she needs. Once she puts her name to paper there is no room for second thoughts, and she is no Minnie MacBride. She has many roads open to her. She is pulled in three ways at the same time — this farm on the mainland, a house waiting for her in Boston and the island that everybody can see her heart is stuck in. She needs time. Maybe she needs help.' But Susan hid her mind no longer. She spoke out now. She was going to Boston. Hughie's people and her own wanted her and she would make that her choice. So she has something deeper down in her mind. But the

114

T.D. was not as used to the dark mind of the island and he kept nagging at her to be guided by him. She lost patience with him and lashed him with words as near as no matter to Conal Andy's. It was not she he had in mind but the buckos with the money he had in tow. She was as shameless in the way she stormed at him as Mary Jim was at the students, and people murmured against her. She was going too far and she was not really saying what was still hidden. The T.D. was quick to sense their mood. 'There you are Johnny Anthon, that's the thanks I get after the way I put myself out to help this woman. And you stand there like a dummy and let her throw every last word of scorn in her head at me.' It was Conal Andy who spoke. 'I say Amen to every word she said. You carry the story to the playboys in Dublin that turned their backs on the people that put them where they are.' Johnny Anthon sought to go a step with Conal Andy and then take the sting out of his words. There was no gainsaying that the talk in the jails made sense to Hughie and that what made sense to him and those with him there went far beyond what was done when the men they trusted got their hands on the helm. But a man in jail could be a bit like a man lying awake at night. Many a time he got a thing into his head at night and it made sense to him then and he had to laugh at himself come daylight. A T.D. had a lot to put up with, but God fits the back for the burden and a T.D. had to grow a thick skin. Johnny Anthon had nothing more on his mind than to take Susan's side. The wise thing for the T.D. would be to leave things as they were. Now that everything was out there was no telling what might come of further talk among themselves. To

his way of thinking Susan's mind had more of
Hughie in it than herself and she might yet be got
to see that. She might still make another choice.
Hughie was a smart man and if little heed was put
in his ideas at the time people were more and more
going back to what he said now; likely Susan more
than anybody. There was more and more talk against
Government gifts. An island couldn't live on scraps.
Sometimes Johnny Anthon came near to saying the
same thing himself. If a few words of Hughie's
could keep nagging at him was it any wonder
Susan had so much of them in her? 'You are guessing Johnny Anthon.' Susan broke in, 'and you're
doing good guessing but there is more of Hughie
in me than his talk. Hughie was a proud man, I have
to bear that in mind, a modest man, a quiet man
for a man who had no need to be quiet for he had
the strength of a spring tide in him, but above all
a proud man. No prouder.'

This lengthy speech roused the T.D. He made
one last try. He stood up on a chair. 'Does anybody
see sense in Susan's people in Boston wasting money
on tickets when it all can be saved, with a bit over
for herself, if she puts her name to this piece of
paper?' Nobody spoke. Johnny Anthon rid his
throat and the T.D. turned to him hopefully but
Conal Andy rasped in his word while Johnny
Anthon was scratching his beard. If there was one
time when Susan must speak for herself this was it.
'I know my mind and I know the mind of Hughie's
people in Boston. Put your paper in your pocket.'
An angry T.D. elbowed his way to the door.

17

Smoke rose from the grey flags on the mainland. Somebody wise in the ways of the island was calling for a boat. Conal Andy and his sons had all but finished putting away their morning's catch of lobsters in a floating storage tank. Men on The Green called to them and pointed. Who could it be? But then it was equal who it was. Smoke from the grey flags must be heeded. Conal Andy himself sat on the tiller. His sons rowed.

Two girls came lightly down the rocks. It was only when they greeted Conal Andy by name that he saw in these two well dressed young women the tomboys in trousers with packs on their backs that were part of the great upset over *No Trespass*. 'Well I'm damned but you are a pair of as fine looking girls as I ever laid an eye on,' Conal Andy said, and the girls, chuckling, hopped aboard. They even knew the christian names of Conal Andy's two sons. 'How is Susan', one of them asked and their gay greeting sobered. 'Ach, poor Susan,' Conal Andy said. He made no mention of her plan to leave the island. His sons were silent too. For a full minute there was only the faint click of the oars in the rowlocks and the swish of the water along the sides of the boat.

'We will somehow have to hold back the tears for the children are sure to be there at this hour,' one of the girls said. Conal Andy's sons turned to meet their father's glance. So Susan had warned them. Had they some reason for coming? Without the need of words, Conal Andy and his sons held counsel. There was enough mystery about Susan abroad on the island not to add to it by a whisper that the girls were up to something. Conal Andy flicked a match against his thumbnail. 'Susan has her mind made up to go to Boston' he said. Both girls looked down at their hands. Conal Andy and his sons had a chance for a less hurried glance. So the girls knew. There was no doubt they knew, and their silence could only mean that they were a bit taken aback that the others knew too. 'Her people are in Boston,' one of the girls said. There was no further talk for a minute or two. To be sure Susan was a good hand with a pen and there was no day without a bundle of letters, so it was not strange that she should have written to the students or that the girls who slept in her house should wish to say good-bye.

'It's a wonder the boys didn't come too,' Conal Andy said. It was partly a probe and partly an honest wish that they should have come back at a time when the island could have made them welcome. 'Many a time we laughed at ourselves for making strangers of you.' 'They wanted to come,' one of the girls said and again they both looked down at their hands and one stole a side look at the other as though nervous she had said too much. 'They would have been welcome' was all Conal Andy said. A seagull glided low overhead. A cormorant

broke surface with a fish in her beak. Conal Andy's
sons put more weight on their oars. Another boat
came within hailing distance, Big Jim and one of
Paddy Brian's sons with three lobster pots they
were changing hopefully to other known lobster
haunts. Big Jim left the talking to the others at
first, but one of the girls made it clear she knew
who he was. 'We won't cause so much upset this
time' she said. 'A lot of things have changed since
you were here before. You know it was over our
crew . . . . .' Big Jim broke off and shook a bowed
head. 'We know. You would have done the same
thing if Hughie was in danger. Nobody is to blame.
Susan made that clear in all her letters to us.' One
of the girls was ready-tongued and she spoke
earnestly. 'It was hardest on Mary' Big Jim said
sadly. 'She blamed herself that it was her talk drove
me to try a second shot. It was not, though I did
have in mind the need we were in.' 'You can't live
by the sea like we do' Conal Andy cut in, 'but it
will snatch somebody every so often. This time it
was the island's best crew that was snatched.' 'But
a crew would have to believe in itself to risk itself
for others. It was a brave thing that was done. It
makes us glad and sad to say that we knew such
men.' 'You said it girl, it was a brave thing that
was done. That is what will be talked about by the
firesides, the bravery and not the drowning. That's
what gives an island the heart to live on.' Sometimes it takes something to happen to open a
person's eyes.' Big Jim said quietly. The boats
separated. It was the silent one of the two girls
now spoke. 'So long as a man doesn't pity himself
it's no harm for him to ask himself did he do
wrong; I mean man or woman.' 'It beats all that a

119

girl like you can see so deep into life,' Conal Andy said thoughtfully. 'What are you but a child.' 'Maybe young people always had sense and that it is only now they can make themselves heard.' Conal Andy's sons laughed. 'You should give a mission to the island,' one of them said. 'Your sermons would cause more of an uproar than *No Trespass.* I would like to hear Johnny Anthon coming out from one of them. One thing certain, Mary Jim would be on your side this time.' 'Mary Jim's sermon was not wasted either,' one of the girls said. 'Tell her that, if we don't get the chance.' Talk was now in a lighter mood. The girls could ask about this person and that. 'This time we can't have a dance,' one of Conal Andy's boys said. 'There will be no dance on the island, nor will one from the island go to a dance outside before twelve months are passed.' 'Unless I miss my guess it won't be long before there is not the makings of a dance left on the island,' Conal Andy said. 'But won't the island live as long as it has Poolban?' It was Conal Andy's turn to be now taken aback — talk like this didn't come by chance from a girl who had spent only a few days on the island. 'Listen to me girl and be open with me. Is it the way the island flows in and out of Poolban that makes Susan say 'no' to the T.D. about selling?' One girl glanced at the other. 'We can tell you the truth about that — Poolban or no Poolban Susan would not sell.' 'Thank God for that,' Conal Andy said looking skywards.

There was a gathering of people on The Green. drawn there to see who it was knew enough to light a fire on the flags. Kitty Paddy Brian was among them. Conal Andy lowered his voice. 'If

120

there's more to your coming than you let out so far and that you would not wish to let out yet, mind yourselves to Kitty. If you drop a stitch she'll soon pick you up.'

There was a warm welcome from both men and women for the girls. Susan's children, unsure until their names were called, ran forward with upraised arms. Susan was on their heels. She embraced one girl after the other and then all three with arms linked, the children dancing around them, went inside. Susan shut the door behind her. In broad daylight with neighbour women still on The Green this was as clear a hint as shutting the door in their faces. 'Well', Kitty gasped, 'talk about *No Trespass.*' Not even Mary Jim could take Susan's side this time. Kitty had her say. She could make no sense of the girls coming back to the island. A body could say it was natural enough their coming if everything was open about it. But why was the door shut? There had to be some hidden meaning. What could there be to hide now with Susan saying straight out that she was going to Boston?

Could it be that the students were here to argue her out of that? Nobody could be sure who first thought of this but once it was said Kitty fastened on it and Mary Jim too. They were sure this must be the girls' errand, but noise was all Kitty and Mary Jim had in common for it was Kitty's prayer that the girls might have their way this time, while Mary Jim was as ready as no matter to let fly like on that other night. Why couldn't their kind keep their noses out of other peoples business? Little would make her walk in and put it up to them to say straight out what their errand was. Nobody said with her and she kept her place on The Green.

Johnny Anthon put in his word. It would be his wish, like Kitty's that Susan would go back on what she said about leaving. It was his hope that she was only caught up in anger that could fade and maybe talk with the girls would do it. The T.D. was not without his share of blame. He should have known enough to keep out of Susan's way. Maybe the island was not entirely free either. It could be that enough had not been done to make Susan see everybody would stand behind her. But Kitty found a way to raise a doubt. If Susan's mind was not for going to Boston would she say what she said about being sorry that the sods to cover Hughie's grave were not cut from the turf on The Green where the children played? That could only come into a body's mind looking back at the grave from Boston. The like was never heard on the island. If her mind was that firm nothing would shake it, so what was going on behind the closed door?

They were a shade taken aback when the door opened at the height of their talk and Susan stepped out and rid her throat in a way that was as good as if she called out 'listen here.' Even men at work straightened their backs and turned with the others to face her. All that was needed was one glance to tell everybody that she was about to say whatever it was she had withheld. The girl students came into the doorway. 'I have to ask you all not to think too hard of me but I had to make sure I was doing as Hughie would wish and that was something I had to sort out myself. Nobody could help me. It was easy to give in to go to Boston but how I left here was not so simple. It came to me all of a sudden what I had to do and the more I thought of it the surer I was that I was right. I told you I was going to Boston but I did not say I had the tickets already. They came without an American stamp for the Anchor Line sent them so they passed through the Post Office without raising any talk. They came in this,' She held up a large envelope. 'Now the time is here when I have to speak and I am afraid. I would like the word to go out that I want you all to gather in on my floor as soon as I get the children to sleep. It's the lanthorn I will light and I'll set it before the window. When you see the light won't you all come in?" They nodded without speaking. 'What I have to say is not a thing I would like to have to say twice.' Her voice shook. Nobody spoke and the silence tightened. In the end it was Johnny Anthon who spoke. 'It will be as you say, Susan. As soon as the light shows in your window every grown up body on the island will be in on your floor.' Her glance went from face to face. She turned and walked slowly back. 'I have an idea we won't like it Conal Andy,' Paddy Brian said. It was the first time he had been the spokesman for the trio but nobody noticed. 'Like it or not, Paddy, nobody will gainsay her.' Johnny Anthon flicked a match and lit Conal Andy's pipe and his own.

The neighbours gathered at nearby gables and as soon as light shone in the window they made for the open door. Johnny Anthon led the way in. No one tried to find a seat. The few chairs on the floor were pushed aside to make more standing room. Women clustered inside the door and pushed their men forward. Johnny Anthon, Conal Andy and Paddy Brian were nudged to the front. Men were in their working clothes but women were dressed as for a station or for a wake except that they were

without their shawls. Susan stood by the recessed
bed. The girl students had their backs to the room
door. No man lit his pipe. 'I must have been a trial
to you all holding back on you as I did,' Susan
began quietly. 'But I know what I am going to
say would only upset you, but I have to say it
now for I am going out from the island in the
morning.' 'In the morning.' There was not a person
in the kitchen that did not add a breath to the
gasp. 'In the morning,' she said again. She turned
to the girls by the room door. 'They will go with
me and see me and the children on the Derry boat.'
She smiled gently. 'I know you must have your
tongues well sharpened against me.' 'All we had
against you, Susan and I may as well out with it,
was the way you kept everything to yourself. What
need had you to keep your mind hid from us?'
Kitty said softly. 'Because of what I had on it,
Kitty, for I have more to tell you than that I am
leaving the island in the morning. 'But your place'
Kitty probed, 'what about your place? Did you
settle with somebody about that? We all know
what you think about the T.D. but don't cut
off your nose to spite your face. Did you do
better for yourself than he offered?'

'I'm not selling the house or land to anybody.'
For the first time she raised her voice and her
head. 'But it makes no sense, and the island won't
stand by and let you hurt yourself.' Kitty pushed
her way forward and the kitchen let her have her
say again. 'There's still time — a boat could go
out and the T.D. would be in like a flash with a
paper for you to sign. The money could follow
you.'

Susan shook her head. 'I'm not selling Kitty.'

That's why I kept my mind to myself for so long. I had to be sure. I had to bear in mind the kind of man Hughie was.' But Kitty would not give up. 'You heard what was said when Minnie MacBride went and how we agreed the soot seeps, in a slimy patch, through the cold chimney, and weeds soon eat into thatch. Minnie's house was saved but how long will the shine last on yours? This other man the T.D. spoke of, he would make a castle of it.'

'But would it then be Duffy's of Poolban, part of the island?' Susan challenged.

Kitty gave up. 'Have it your way and let the soot and the weeds have theirs.'

'I could not thole to think of this house going that way that's why there is a two gallon tin of paraffin oil at the back door. When I go out from here in the morning I want this house set on fire.' 'No.' It was partly a gasp, partly a sob. Kitty alone was roused to anger. She elbowed her way to the front again. 'This is more of it, Susan Duffy. You keep your mind under a cloud and all of a sudden you hit us with this squall. Whatever did we do to you that you make little of us in this way?'

'No woman ever had better neighbours, Kitty, and no woman ever thought more of her neighbours. If only you knew what I went through . . . . . .' her voice crumbled.

'We know, Susan,' Kitty said gently. Nobody was going to make little of Kitty by cutting in on her now. 'Many a tear we dropped for you, but this . . . . . .' A helpless Kitty eased herself back among the others. But Susan had a grip on herself again. 'I know you have been talking about me and you had every right but this was a thing only Hughie

125

and me could settle.' For the first time she smiled 'I'm not going astray in the head. I went over and over in my mind the kind of man Hughie Duffy was and how the people he trusted hurt him. He wasn't one to talk but we were always open with one another, Hughie and me. It would be his wish the island to set fire to this house before the hearth cools and the soot shows.'

Kitty had one more try. 'Speak to her can't you, Johnny Anthon. Have you lost your tongue? Tell her the island will not raise a hand to do what she has in mind.'

One of the student girls came to Susan's side. 'The boys wanted to come to take this work off the island's hands,' she said. 'Do you hear me, Johnny Anthon,' Kitty struggled.

'I hear you, Kitty.' His voice was so low it was almost a whisper. He turned to Conal Andy and Paddy Brian but they were no help to him. 'You are hard on us, Susan.' It was only the quietness of the kitchen let him be heard. He took a firm step forward and faced his neighbours. 'This is a proud thought Susan thought, but it will only lead to a proud deed if the island itself does the burning. Susan knows it would only bring shame on us if she let anybody but us do it. That's why she said no to the boys. This house with its scorched walls will still be Duffy's of Poolban. People up and down the bay and beyond will see it and say it. And I make this vow: while God leaves me the strength of my four bones this house will get its coat of whitewash every year. Maybe when the island is dead, for it will likely empty itself on Susan's heels, the four walls will serve as its tombstone for many a day. I know I won't sleep for a month

126

after it but I'll do my share of the burning in the morning. All of it if I have to.' 'You won't have to Johnny Anthon,' Conal Andy said harshly. Every man on the floor signalled with a nod that he would help.

'Big Jim and one of Paddy Brian's boys will row us to the station in the morning. The girls made the offer, and I was glad of it, to go with me to Derry.'

'Thank God for your choice of a crew to row you out,' Kitty said and wiped her eyes with her apron. 'There is little more to say,' Susan took up. She turned to Johnny Anthon. 'I didn't light the lamp, so the globe would not be hot,' she handed him the bowl and gave the globe to Conal Andy. That was their Sunday night way. 'And now I have to ask the help of all you. I have to leave the island dry-eyed because of the children; they are not leaving the island but going to meet their aunties and uncles. There is only one way I can do that. Let there be no good-bye. The Green had best be empty when I cross it. Ah! that Green. My heart will often come back to it — to dance. I had more than my share of joy and now, what can I say but, God Bless you all.' For a moment there was no sound.

Down by the weather door a woman swooned. 'Get her to the fresh air,' Kitty bustled. 'We would all be the better of a mouthful.' It made it easier now for the kitchen to empty itself out. Susan stood stock still, her arms tight across her breast and watched them go. Johnny Anthon, Conal Andy, and Paddy Brian let the others out ahead of them. Clear of the doorway they paused. 'We had as well get the lamp to Kitty for safe keeping' Johnny

Anthon said. Paddy Brian led the way. Conal Andy, holding the globe high, was last. There were no voices on the paths.